Aoirei
青い霊

Ranajay Das

ISBN-13: 978-981-11-7921-1

For my family
For MaryAnn
For my friends
For my MCW coach
For the wonderful people in ECI
For everyone who bought this book an supported my dream
For myself

Thank you

Table of Contents

1. Memory

There's a theory that we often misremember past events, superimposing the present onto the past to fill in the blanks that our minds have forgotten.

I don't remember much of my childhood. There are some memories that come back in fragments; and when I let my mind relax, they become whole. Sometimes these memories are triggered by a song or a smell or something I see. Are these just fabrications of my mind to fill in the blanks? Or did they really happen? The harder I try to remember, the sleepier I get, so I just let the memories come when they want to.

I'm four years old, maybe five. I'm standing on a train platform. The platform is crowded.

I'm not alone.

I'm holding on to someone's hand. I squeeze it and the hand squeezes back. This is my mother's hand.

The air around us is cold and I see my breath come out in puffs of white in front of me. I turn to look behind me and the world goes still. There is an old lady looking at me. She has a blue orb of flame on top of her head. She's wearing a yukata. Her clothes have no colour, much like the rest of her. Everything about her is a shade of grey, save for the pale blue flame. Her smile is benevolent and it fills me with a feeling of warmth.

And then time starts up again. I hear the hustle and bustle around me. I feel a tug on my arm and I look up to see my mother's face. Before she can turn her head to look at me, everything goes blank.

That's what I remember. In college, I watched an anime movie called *Escaflowne*. It's nowhere as good as the TV show but that's not the point. There's a scene in the movie where the protagonist, as a child, is waiting at the railway station. Just like in my memory, time stops and she sees an ethereal figure looking at her. Watching that scene, my own forgotten memory of the train platform came rushing back in for the first time. Did my mind fabricate it on the spot to fill in the blanks left in my childhood?

Why does it feel so real then?

Doctor Zhao reminds me that I have mild schizophrenia. I don't recall when I was diagnosed but I've been taking antipsychotics for my condition ever since I can remember. Sometimes I have trouble discerning my real memories from fabricated ones. I feel that some of my memories aren't even mine because they seem like they're from an era long, long ago. Someone planting seeds in a field, or small hands folding paper shapes in a forest, or large hands holding cigarettes under a mango tree. They feel like they don't belong to me. Jojo says some of them don't.

There are weeks when I'm really depressed and I stop taking my medication. That's when I start seeing them…the people with the blue orbs of flame on top of their heads. I don't see them often and a lot of that may have to do with the fact that I don't like going out in public. My work usually involves sitting at home and coding. But when I'm sitting in my veranda, smoking or going to the food court for dinner, I'll sometimes notice a faint tinge of blue, weaving silently through the crowds. They look like regular people who are going about their day, except that they're devoid of any colour; like a black and white photograph that decided to leave its picture frame and go about the task of buying fruits or flowers or whatever it is that black and white photographs do in their free time. They're hard to notice and if it weren't for the blue orb of flame atop their heads, they might as well have been a part of the background.

Doctor Zhao gets upset when I mention them because it probably means that I was off my meds (which is usually the case). In spite of that, she says that it's very important that I keep her informed about the "colourless blue people" I see.

Who did you see this time, Kiku?

Was it someone you knew or had seen before in real life?

Did they resemble someone you met recently?

Did they talk to you?

Did you talk to them?

How do you feel when you see them?

Why do you suppose they're black and white?

How long had you not taken your medication when you first saw them this week?

Are you being honest with me, Kiku?

So many questions. At times like these I bury myself deep in the task of watching TV shows and anime. There's such blissful sense of escapism in anime. Sometimes I feel like Shinji from *Neon Genesis Evangelion*—no memories of his mother and strained relationship with his father. I wonder when my own father will invite me to ride a giant robot into battle, like Shinji. Other times I feel like Sato from the anime *Welcome to the N.H.K.*—a hikikomori[1] who thinks that the N.H.K. has conspired to keep him from connecting with people and they're the reason that he's a shut-in. I have the colourless blue people to blame for that…perhaps. I don't remember.

Doctor Zhao says that I should leave my house more often. Travel more. Interact with people. Stop being such a recluse. I've been saving up money for a while now to travel to Japan. I've never been there before but I feel an intense connection with the country which is difficult to explain. There's a lot of darkness inside me. A change of environment might be what I need to shine some light on those dark places. Or maybe, I just don't want to be in Singapore any more.

I don't want to be here—being myself.

Doctor Zhao made me promise not to skip my meds while I'm there.

You know what they say about promises, laughs Jojo.

---

[1] *Hikikomori*—Literally "pulling inward, being confined", i.e., "acute social withdrawal". They are reclusive adolescents or adults who withdraw from social life, often seeking extreme degrees of isolation and confinement.

2. Chikyumisaki

Jin had never been to Muroran before. It was rare for his parents to take him anywhere besides his grandmother's home in Otaru. He had spent all the seven years of his life shuttling between his grandmother's home and his real home in Sapporo. He didn't mind the travelling. In fact, he enjoyed it! It was a welcome break from the tense and often loud conversations between his mother and father at the dinner table. They didn't fight when they travelled, especially not with people around them. We should always show our best side to the world. Crying and screaming is something you should never do. Even when you feel like crying, you must hold it in. That's the sign of a true man. And Jin wanted to be a true man just like his father.

He had worked hard the whole year to get good grades in his class. They were higher than everyone else. His mother and father were so proud of him. He had done it for them. They had promised to take him somewhere special if he did well in his tests. They had promised to take him to see a beautiful lighthouse in Muroran. It was on a cape called Chikyumisaki—Cape Earth. Jin had never seen a lighthouse before. It sounded magical in the dictionary—

A tower with a powerful light that is built on or near the shore to guide ships away from danger.

In his mind's eye he saw a blue tower of light, reaching up to the heavens. The blue was cold and warm all at once. It was pure. Beyond the light was a vast ocean of darkness. The dark ocean and the dark sky became one and the line of horizon separating them had decided to go on a holiday.

Just like Jin and his parents were doing right now. He had no siblings so he had the back seat of the car all to himself. His father was driving while his mother sat next to his father in the passenger seat. They hadn't fought the whole day. Muroran was a special place for both of them because that's where they had first met, his father had said to him. They passed by farms covered in snow as they travelled south, from Sapporo to Muroran. Along the way they stopped at a couple of highway stops to eat soft serve ice cream and for his father to smoke. Jin loved melon flavoured soft-serve, as did his mother. They shared a single soft-serve at both the stops. He loved his mother very much. She was tall and beautiful and always smelled of roses. He brought his English textbook from tuition school along with him because his mother loved listening to poetry recited by him. She couldn't speak much English herself, so it made the exchanges even more special because his mother would look at him with wide eyes and a beaming smile as he flawlessly recited poem after poem after poem. He had quite the flair for it too and would add flourishes to his voice to make her giggle.

Jin's father on the other hand seemed to show no interest in his talent for English. Jin found it particularly stressful to recite passages to his father who would stare sternly and nod while he read them aloud. The apparent lack of enthusiasm on his father's part always made Jin feel like he was being a burden to him. His father probably liked being left alone. Which is why he would always smoke alone on the balcony. Just like his mother, his father was a tall and thin man. He wore round glasses with black rims. Jin feared his father but he also deeply respected him. After all, he was showing him how to become a true man. Always show your best side to the world. Don't cry even when you feel like it. And most importantly, don't be a burden.

He had nothing to worry about today though because he was very far from sadness. The journey of three hours felt like it had lasted for an eternity. They were in Muroran now and driving up the steep, snow covered road that led to the lighthouse. He went from one side of the back seat to the other, absorbing all the sights to the left and the right of him. His father threw him a quick glance and Jin stopped darting about and sat down quietly behind his father's seat. It wasn't too late in the afternoon, but the skies were completely grey and covered in clouds. It was snowing lightly outside. They had arrived at Chikyumisaki.

Jin ran out of the car and climbed up the steps that led to a landing where the public toilet was. He gestured to his mother and father with his hands, urging them to climb up faster. They both chuckled, even his father.

"Wait for us here, Jin. Don't go anywhere without us, ok?" his father instructed as he reached the landing and headed for the toilet. Jin nodded dutifully, barely able to contain his excitement. His mother waited outside with him.

"Are you excited, Jin-chan[2]?" his mother asked.

"Yes! I want to see the lighthouse!" replied an enthusiastic Jin.

"Do you want me to tell you a secret about the lighthouse?"

"Yes!"

"Promise, you won't tell your father I told you this?"

"I promise!"

His mother paused and took a deep breath, inhaling the cold winter air.

"I used to live in Muroran. When I was in high school, every week I would come to the lighthouse to write haiku. I wanted to become a poet you see and the lighthouse is a peaceful place to be with your own thoughts and nature. One day, while I was writing, I saw a tall young man looking at me. It was your father. He still wears the same glasses that he wore that day. He came and sat by me and asked me about my poetry. He was very handsome, just like you, Jin-chan."

Jin giggled at the comparison and then blushed.

"Looking at your father made my heart beat faster. I asked him why I had never seen him before and he replied that he was from Sapporo. He had come here on a graduation trip with his friends but had decided to be by himself on that day. We couldn't stop talking and time just flew by. Later that evening I snuck into the lighthouse with him. That's why this place is special to us, Jin-chan. This is where you were made. And had it not been for you, I would've never met your father for a second time. Do you understand?"

---

[2]*Chan*—A suffix in Japanese, often attached to children's names when calling them by their given names. It can also be attached to kinship terms in a childish language. It may also be used for babies, young children, and teenage girls, lovers or close friends.

Jin didn't understand, but nodded along anyway. He was the reason his parents were together and that thought filled him with warm satisfaction.

"Jin", his father suddenly called out, "come and read this!"

Jin went inside the toilet. His father was pointing to a sign. "Read the English part, Jin", his father instructed excitedly.

"Beware of lost items!" read out Jin.

His father chuckled and Jin chuckled along with him without knowing why. He had never seen his father this happy before. He didn't even know that his father knew how to be happy. The thought made his chuckle turn into laughter. Both father and son laughed wildly. His mother entered the men's toilet too to see what all the commotion was about. His father pointed to the sign and kept laughing. His mother didn't understand what the sign said in English, but could read the Japanese words on top of it. She laughed too as she said to them that they were both lost and that she would leave them behind in the toilet. All three of them laughed out loud and had there been anyone else at Cape Chikyu on that day, they would've seen a family that had lost their minds, standing inside the men's toilet, laughing to their heart's content.

The snow had subsided outside. The family made its way, hand in hand, to the top of the observatory. Jin broke away and ran to the railings at the edge. Before him stretched out a calm azure sea and a cloudy, grey sky. He could see where the sky met the sea, but the line wasn't straight. It was curved, like the surface of the earth. Columns of sunlight pierced through the clouds and lit up the sea in patches of golden light. The lights shimmered and glistened. Jin saw the shapes of birds and dinosaurs in this tapestry created on the surface of the sea. He looked to his left and saw the lighthouse on a piece of land jutting out from below the cape. It wasn't a column of blue light, like he had imagined it to be, but a small white tower with large windows and a white dome on top of it. It stood pure and erect, glistening in another column of sunlight that had broken through the clouds. He looked at it, mesmerised.

His parents joined him and let out exaggerated exclamations as they pointed to the sea and the sky. They stood together for a while, his mother and father, holding each other's hands behind him, not saying a single word and just letting themselves absorb the scenery and the memories that hide in special places like this.

"Did you bring the condoms?"

"Yes, they're in my purse."

"Want to go to the lighthouse?"

"Are you crazy? It's covered in snow and the staircase leading down to it is locked. Besides, we can't leave Jin-chan here by himself."

"He's a big boy. He can take care of himself."

"I'm not going to the lighthouse, please."

"Ok, how about the bathroom then? There's no one here today."

"And what about Jin-chan?"

"You'll be fine here by yourself, won't you, Jin?" Jin's father asked him. It was more of a statement than a question.

Jin nodded, not quite following their conversation.

"See?"

"It doesn't feel right."

"Think about why we came here. Think about our marriage."

Silence.

"Ok. But we must hurry. I don't want to leave him out here alone for too long."

"I doubt it will take long. It's been a while, as you know."

"Let's not start that conversation again. Let's go now before either of us says something that we'll regret", his mother said.

"Fine. Fine. Now you be a good boy and stay here, ok Jin? Don't go anywhere", his father told him.

"I won't", he promised.

His father gave him a stern look. Don't be a burden, the look said.

His mother and father walked hurriedly down the stairs to the toilet. Jin fixed his gaze back at the curved horizon. He wondered what made it curved and not straight.

CAW!

Jin turned to his right to see a crow that was looking at him inquisitively. Jin crowed back at the crow.

"Caw", the crow said.

"Caw", replied Jin.

The crow flapped its wings and flew over Jin's head to land on the gate that led to the lighthouse.

Jin looked at the crow.

The crow looked back at Jin.

"I will eat you", the crow said.

Jin frowned. Why would the crow say something like that? The crow flapped its wings again and jumped in its spot on the gate. Jin started walking towards the crow. The crow tilted its head and looked at him quizzically. It flapped its wings a few more times before launching into flight. It flew towards the lighthouse. Jin trudged through the snow and stopped at the gate; it had a rusty old lock on it. The snow was high enough for him to climb over easily and his body was light enough to not fall through the snow. With one foot over the gate, he looked back at the toilet his parents had gone into. He looked ahead at the golden, shimmering lighthouse. His other foot climbed over the gate and before he knew it, he was on the other side. It was a winding path down to the lighthouse and Jin was careful not to go too fast. His eyes were searching for the crow that wanted to eat him. He wanted to ask the crow why. He reached the lighthouse and walked all around its circumference.

CAW!

He looked above him. His eyes met the crow's who was looking down at him from atop the lighthouse.

"How do I get up there?" Jin asked the crow.

"Use the door", the crow replied.

Jin circled back to the door of the lighthouse. Its handle was too high for him to reach.

"I can't reach the handle."

"Not that door", the crow said.

Jin didn't understand. There weren't any other doors into the lighthouse. He looked around him and all he saw was snow and walls. He was too short to peer over them. Maybe there was a door below the lighthouse? He circled the lighthouse again looking for a staircase that led down but there was nothing. He noticed that some snow had piled up near one of the walls. He climbed up the snow to see if he could get a better view of the side of the lighthouse that was below him. He looked over the wall and saw the beautiful sea again, azure blue spotted with gold. He looked below and saw the sea crashing gently against the black rocks. No doors yet.

CAW, Jin heard just behind him, louder than before. As he turned around, the crow flew straight at his face, claws outstretched. Jin instinctively stepped back. But instead of solid ground, his foot found nothing but air. He tumbled into the light, trying to grab on to its golden rays. But all he grabbed was the wind. The last thing Jin saw before he plunged to his death, were large dark wings that blocked out the whole world.

Rain falls to be snow

Snow falls to become the rain

The wind keeps blowing

3. 誰

My feet are heavy, but my soul feels light.

I've been walking for hours exploring the suburbs of Asakusabashi. It's August in Tokyo and it's been raining ever since I got here. Amidst the glow of the rows of vending machines that line the narrow streets and the soft pouring rain, I find myself blissfully lost. I'm smiling stupidly to myself. There aren't that many people on the streets. The rain is pitter-pattering atop the black umbrella I borrowed from the hostel I'll be spending the next four nights in.

Everything is glistening in the rain. The street lamps, the traffic lights, the lights from the vending machines, they all reflect off the black sheen of water on the road. It's chilly and I'm glad to have brought my black weatherproof jacket along with me. I've passed by rows and rows of houses, tiny ramen shops and even the tiniest laundromat I have ever seen in my life which only had a single washing machine and a dryer. And electricity poles. Everywhere! Supporting millions of overhead cables, twisting and winding through miles of urban landscape. A superterranean labyrinth of energy floating above our plane of existence.

It's fascinating what a change of scenery can do to you. Just last week I was grumbling about the muggy rain of Singapore, and here I am now, awestruck by the shimmering lights reflecting off cramped, rain drenched streets in a different country; somewhere far away from everyone and everything I know. I walk past some children returning home who silently half-bow to me as they pass by me. They look like siblings, a young boy holding a tiny umbrella for his sister, both wearing yellow ponchos that cover them completely, including their backpacks. The boy glances back at me quickly before continuing. I've noticed people stealing glances at me in this neighbourhood. Is it because I have brown skin? Maybe they're not used to seeing people of colour around here.

As I ponder upon the homogeneity of Japan and the location of my hostel—which I seem to have strayed too far away from—I feel a gust of cold wind hit me square in the face. I am standing in front of a shrine. There's a large stone torii gate that marks the entrance to it. It doesn't seem to be a particularly important shrine but the amount of space dedicated to it in the middle of all these houses is surprising. The entire shrine is surrounded by a thicket of tall trees. Further inside I see a white pillared temizuya[3] with a black tiled roof and a dark wooden building behind it which must be the altar. The air is damp with the smell of rain and freshly fallen leaves. I cross the road and step through the torii gate. The air grows colder around me. It's a familiar coldness. I'm unsure if I'm supposed to be here at night, but since there aren't any locked gates or ropes to tell me otherwise, I make my way to the temizuya to wash my hands. The rain has died down and I can hear the gentle flow of the water in the water basin and the rustling of the leaves around me. I've read that you're supposed to wash both your hands, your mouth and the wooden ladle at the basin to purify yourself before approaching the altar. As I set my umbrella down to pick up the ladle, I see a blue glow coming from the altar.

It's one of them.

I feel a slight pain in the core of my chest. Did it see me? I don't mind seeing them in crowded places. It's only when I'm alone that I don't want to run into them. The blue glow flickers like a flame. I slowly put down the ladle and start to turn around.

"誰[4]?"

I freeze.

Nope. Nope. Didn't hear a thing. I briskly walk the fuck out of the shrine and onto the streets. My heart is pounding and I can feel the cold air on the beads of sweat that are forming on my face. My brisk walk sways into a full-fledged sprint. Something rumbles overhead. The lights dancing on the streets turn into a blur as my eyes are unable to focus on anything. I

---

[3] *Temizuya*—A *chōzuya* or *temizuya* (手水舎) is a Shinto water ablution pavilion for a ceremonial purification rite known as temizu.
[4] *誰 (Dare)*—Who

don't stop running until I reach the banks of Sumida River, which cuts through Tokyo into the Tokyo Bay. Panting for breath I grab onto the railings along the river bank. As I look across to the lights on the other side of the river, I have a sick feeling that the voice I heard is about to run straight through me, laughing.

Fuck! You cheating ghost! You're not allowed to run through objects! Jojo objects.

I jolt my head around but there's no one behind me. Nothing ran through me. It was just my imagination. I start laughing at the ridiculousness of it all. I'm probably having one of my non-medicated episodes again, confusing fabricated memories with my own. Did I even hear a woman's voice at the shrine asking me something in Japanese? Doubtful. I'm confusing reality with fantasy.

I look around to see couples walking along the river hand in hand. No one pays me any attention. I find a bench to sit down and smoke. The cigarettes in Japan are way cheaper than Singapore and I'm going to use this opportunity to smoke my lungs to death. My hands shake as I take a cigarette out of the soft pack, but soon they calm down. Across the water is probably Ryogoku, where the sumo wrestling stadium is, but all I see right now are the twinkling yellow lights all along the river. A cool, gentle breeze dances across its surface, bringing with it the smell of fish. I'm feeling hungry.

I stub my cigarette out on the bottom of my shoe and walk back towards the suburbs as it starts to rain again.

4. Nakamura-san

Nakamura-san is trapped inside his own apartment. He has tried everything he can to leave. He tried the door knob that doesn't turn. He tried opening the window that won't open. He slammed his numb fists onto the walls, doors and every inch of the apartment, screaming to be let out, but no one answered. As dust gathers on the tiny kitchen counter in the tiny apartment, so does the dust of despair gather on Nakamura-san's heart. He doesn't sleep any more, nor is he awake. He just is. In and out of time. Like a forgotten souvenir from an overseas trip that sits in the display cabinet, serving no other purpose than to fill space and gather dust.

He has had several roommates over the years, but no one stays. No one speaks to him. No one listens. All he wants is to be let out. Sometimes he gets so frustrated that he knocks things off the tiny dining table in a fit of rage. That's usually when his roommates have had enough of him and start making phone calls to property agents. It's a repetitive cycle.

Sometimes he wonders if this is his own apartment or if this is purgatory. What has he done to deserve this, he often cries. When he looks out of the solitary window, he only sees snow. It's always snowing.

Always snowing.

Always white.

Always snowing.

Always white.

Always snowing.

Always white.

He curls up into a ball and cries dry tears. There is darkness inside and white outside. And in between the black and the white, there is blue.

5. Abashiri Prison

It's 12:18pm when the train pulls into Abashiri station. I've been travelling north. From Tokyo, I've flown all the way up to beautiful Hokkaido. There are rivers and lakes, farms and highways, mountains and beautiful skies. There aren't that many people here as compared to Tokyo and that makes me feel unburdened. From time to time, I see the blue people going about their business, waiting at the railway crossings for the train to pass or wading through farms. They blend in and out of the scenery, never feeling out of place. I've been more aware of them since I arrived in Hokkaido. I count back and realize that I've been off my medication for fourteen days now. It's been fourteen days since I left Singapore.

I didn't make an itinerary for myself before I arrived in Japan. I saved up a lot of money for this trip so that I don't have to worry about fixed schedules. Everything here has been spur-of-the-moment. Everything here is natural. It's as if my heart already knows where it wants to wander.

Today it has brought me to Abashiri. I don't know much about this place. There's a prison from the Meiji era here that has been converted into a prison museum. In the winters, people come here to see drift ice, floating all the way from Russia to Japan across the sea of Okhotsk.

"Today's Abashiri is an unattractive modern town filled with the implements and smells of its largest industry, fishing", says Wikitravel.

Far be it from me to judge a place without having fully explored it, but everything about Abashiri station and the road outside says—unremarkable. I have booked a cheap hotel close to the railway station. The old lady manning the reception doesn't speak much English so we use hand-gestures for much of our brief conversation. I throw in some Japanese words here and there that I've learnt from watching anime. She keeps pointing to a stack of the hotel's business cards—Hotel Moon Abashiri. I have no idea what she's saying, so I just take a card to appease her. I've come to realize that you don't need a great command over the Japanese language to get by in Japan. If you point to what you want, you will eventually get it. And it's the pointing that you will eventually get tired of.

After throwing my luggage into the dingy attic styled room with yellowing wallpaper, I go outside for a smoke. It must've rained here recently because I can smell its sweet dampness in the air. The streets are empty. The occasional car meanders past the front of the hotel, which is supposedly on a main road. Maybe this place sees more people in the winters when tourists come to see the drift ice phenomenon. Perfect—I don't mind the sparseness.

I make my way to the railway station again to buy tickets to the Abashiri prison museum. I mean, I might as well go and take a look at the place, since I'm here. It's a ten minute bus ride, and very soon, the scenery changes from dilapidated town to forests and greenery. I'm the only passenger on the bus which drops me off at the gates of the prison. I stretch my arms and my back. It's so peaceful here. I can hear the chirps of cicadas, buzzing in the air. Higurashi, they're called in Japanese. The only reason I know this word is because of a disturbing anime called *Higurashi—When They Cry*. It's a murder mystery where the characters die gruesome deaths, again and again and again, always falling back into the same cycle. It's not a particularly good anime but you can hear cicadas crying in the background throughout the show.

There's a girl standing just outside the museum entrance—smoking and looking at the sky. She's dressed in an icy blue yukata with azure maple leaf patterns on it. The maple leaves are connected to each other through intertwining blue stems, threading their way through each other, wrapping themselves around the thin frame of the girl. She's not that tall, but her posture is straight and commanding. She lowers her gaze towards me.

Our eyes meet.

I blush and look away. I've never been good at admiring beautiful people because every time they look at me, my mind goes blank. It wasn't just her face that struck me as familiar, even her short brown hair reminded me of a girl I used to like in school.

You wanted to play basketball with her, Jojo remembers.

"That wasn't me", I blurt out louder than I mean to.

I look back at the entrance and see that the girl isn't there. She must've finished her cigarette and gone inside. I walk up to the counter to pay the museum entrance fee and take an English language pamphlet with me.

Opened on July 6th, 1983, Abashiri Prison Museum is operated by the Abashiri Prison Preservation Foundation.

When the full-scale renovation of the Abashiri Prison buildings started in July 1973, Abashiri citizens called for these Meiji era buildings to be relocated and restored as cultural properties. Such sentiment spread broadly and quickly. In response to the citizens' enthusiasm, the first president, Hisahi Sato, and the other members established the foundation on May 28, 1980 and started operating the museum.

The pamphlet goes on to describe the history of how the prison museum came to be and is rather dull and boring. I fold the pamphlet and place it in my jacket's breast pocket. I search for some articles on my phone instead. I come across one by Johannes Schonherr which is particularly interesting—

For almost a century, the town of Abashiri in north-eastern Hokkaido was the location of Japan's most notorious and most feared prison.

Only the most hardened criminals were brought to this forbidding place on the Okhotsk Sea where the harsh winters bring the Siberian drift ice to the shore.

The work was hard, the cells crowded and the wardens were strict and did not tolerate even the tiniest infractions of the rules.

Abashiri stood for the most severe punishment Japanese judges were to hand out short of execution. Crossing the bridge over the Abashiri River to enter the heavily guarded gate in fact meant reaching their final destination for many a brave yakuza, daring robber and reckless outlaw.

Murderers and the like were swiftly executed in those days, they usually did not even start the trek up here. In the early days, anyway.

There are eerie, life-like mannequins scattered throughout the prison compound. Silently, they go about their business of sweeping the floors and planting trees. As I read and walk, I'm aware of the increasing volume of the cicada cries. I look at my watch and its 2:34pm. I have no idea at what time of the day cicadas cry the loudest but something about their crying sounds unsettling to me. In front of me, I see the girl again, turning left inside one of the buildings.

I turn to my pamphlet to see where I am.

At the centre of the radial five-winged prison house is a hexagonal guardhouse. It allows the entire prison to be seen from a single location. The 226 cells, consisting of communal cells and solitary confinement cells, can house 700 prisoners. This was the prison house for 72 years.

I'm suddenly aware of two things—

First, my breath is coming out in clouds of mist, like it does in winter.

Second, the cicada screams are very loud now.

I step across the threshold of the hexagonal guardhouse. All the air inside me rushes out in one long misty breath.

There are blue flames everywhere. Hundreds of them. All along the corridors are streams of blue. And underneath each blue, pulsing orb of flame, is the contorted face of a man with his mouth wide open. Hundreds of contorted faces. Hundreds of contorted bodies. They are grey and naked, naked and grey, save for a white loin cloth around their waists. There's anguish in their faces. Their mouths are wide open.

It wasn't the cicadas that were screaming. It was them.

My mind has gone blank with terror. I'm frozen. My hands are cupping my ears. My mouth is wide open like theirs. I'm screaming without a sound. Their screams are flooding into me. My body is trembling violently.

I don't want to die.

I don't want to die.

I don't want to die.

I don't want to die.

I DON'T WANT TO DIE.

I DON'T WANT TO DIE.

I DON'T WANT TO DIE.

I DON'T WANT TO DIE.

Darkness rushes in. There is only one corridor in front of me now and the light at the end of it is rushing farther and farther away. I can't reach it. I can't move. My body is so tense that at any moment my bones and muscles can snap all at once. I smell mint leaves mixed with blood. The screams are interspersed with the sounds of flapping wings.

Dark wings, flapping all around me.

Flapping.

Cawing.

Biting.

Tearing.

The screams are the screams of a thousand crows as they rip into my flesh. They tear and they tear and they tear until there's nothing left but blackness.

6. Mint Leaves

We are in the Forgotten Forest. I'm holding my mother's hand. I'm not as big as her. I can't walk as fast as her. And yet I love our afternoon walks. The sunlight makes its way down through the sky of leaves. It warms my face and warms my shoulders. A snake comes and greets me good morning. I tell the snake it's already afternoon.

My mother starts singing. I sing along. I don't know the words.

I stretch my arms out to her. She picks me up and places me on her shoulders.

The forest opens up and I can see everything. I see the trees. I see the leaves. I see the ropes. I see the squares I folded for them. I see the birds perching. I see the squirrels fighting. I see the foxes hiding. I see the blue man with four arms riding his buffalo. I see the stars through the sunlight.

The forest and its animals wave at us.

The forest caretakers wave at us.

Their blue souls wink at us.

I wrap my arms around my mother's forehead. I rest my head on top of hers. Her hair smells of mint leaves. I close my eyes and fall asleep.

7. La Porte

I wake up surrounded by yellowing wallpaper and a slanted ceiling. I'm in my hotel room. My whole body is tense and aching as if I just woke up from a fever ridden dream. I don't think it was a bad dream though. I vaguely recollect trees, maybe a forest. And the smell of mint leaves.

Leaves.

Maple Leaves.

They were on that girl's yukata. I shudder as I remember all the screaming faces in the prison. I block it out. I block out their screams. My forehead is aching and my throat is dry. I don't remember if I screamed but I'd rather not remember anything at all.

I search the table next to me for a bottle of water. I must've been very thirsty because I drink the entire bottle in one go. What time is it? I check my watch to see 7:30. Is it morning or evening right now? I unlock my phone and see that it's 7:30pm. I was out cold for at least four hours.

I get out of bed, rubbing my eyes. There's a tiny window in the room that looks out at the railway station. It's raining outside. I go to the bathroom to brush my teeth and wash my face. I still feel muggy so I decide to take a cold shower. Cold showers are the best thing to wake you right up. The sudden jolt of coldness makes you breathe harder and faster and loosens up most knots in your muscles. I scrub my body raw with the loofah I bought from a 100 yen shop in Tokyo. I want to scrub the entire afternoon away. I would, if I could. It was a bad idea to go to the prison. Did I just witness hundreds of ghosts screaming in unison?

Stop it. Block it out.

I keep scrubbing and scrubbing. After I'm done, I wipe myself off with the hotel towel. The towel, like the rest of the hotel, has probably seen better days. There are visible yellow patches on its white surface that I choose to ignore. Ignorance is bliss, a wise man once said. My stomach starts grumbling. Don't ignore me, it pleads. I didn't have lunch today, did I? I change into a fresh set of clothes, pick up my wallet and phone and start to leave.

Suddenly, I realize that I have no idea how I got back to my hotel. Who brought me here? They must've seen the business card I was carrying. I open my wallet and feel around for the business card in one of the hidden flaps. I feel two cards there instead of one. I take both of them out. One of them is the hotel business card I took this afternoon. The other one is a new.

La Porte

Japanese diner

I flip the card over. There's an address in Japanese at the bottom of it. I walk to the reception downstairs and the old lady is kind enough to draw me a map on a piece of paper to show the way from Hotel Moon to La Porte. She seems concerned and asks me—"daijobu desu ka?" a few times. I tell her I'm fine. I borrow an umbrella from her and thank her with a bow. I wonder what kind of state I was in when I was brought back to the hotel. It must've caused quite a stir, judging by her concern.

It's a fifteen minute walk to La Porte. I take my time to enjoy the cold gloomy weather. Abashiri looks a lot better under a blanket of rain. Rain drops pitter-patter on my umbrella. I recall my conversation with the reception lady and realize that I've started to pick up more Japanese phrases. And not just phrases—sometimes during the conversation, I was able to understand what she was saying without knowing what the individual words meant. Was it because she talked in a certain tone that conveyed the meaning better? Maybe I've had a natural talent for learning new languages all along.

Sure you did, Jojo chuckles sarcastically.

Yeah, I know right. I'm getting caught up in my secret delusions of grandeur again.

The rain begins to die down as I turn right, into a smaller lane just before Chuo Park. La Porte is supposed to be somewhere in the alleys behind Abashiri Central Hotel. I fold my umbrella and take my phone out. Phone in one hand, paper in another, I begin the arduous task of navigating the back alleys of Abashiri using my amazing sense of direction. My fifteen minute walk is about to turn into an hour long search. I walk from lane to lane, crisscrossing and retracing my own steps multiple times. I wonder if the reception lady knew where the place was because I can't find it on Google Maps. As I search high and low, one of the shopkeepers asks me what I'm looking for (or I assume that's what she asked me) so I show her the business card for La Porte. She points to a shady looking building at the corner of the street and says—"Force flow". I nod and thank her. There's a sign on the side of the building with the list of establishments inside, and sure enough, one of those establishments is La Porte, on the fourth floor.

I hate the stale smell of cigarette smoke which seems to be a common feature in most Japanese buildings. I'm a smoker myself but I don't understand why people would choose to smoke indoors and have the smell seep into every square inch of a room or a building. This building is no different, if not worse. I'm coughing as soon as I enter the elevator and press the fourth floor button. Some buildings don't have a fourth floor in Japan because the number four is associated with death. The elevator stops at four and opens to a cramped corridor with only one door at the end of it with a sign that says—

La Porte

You have arrived

What a strange sign, I think to myself. I slowly approach the solitary door. Tube lights covered in dead insects flicker above my head. I flinch as I turn the door handle. It's ice cold. The door opens without a sound.

The inside of La Porte is much colder than the outside. The bar counter style restaurant is dimly lit and smells of incense sticks. I'm the only customer. The counter is tiny with only four bar seats so I pick the first one from the left. The kitchen is on the right side and I can hear the clacking of pots and pans inside.

"Irasshaimase[5]", I hear someone call out. I know whose voice it is before I even see her. It's the girl from the prison who was wearing the maple leaf yukata. She's dressed in a black t-shirt and grey denim jeans now. She smiles at me as she walks to the counter. I smirk back.

Trying to act cool huh, Kiku, Jojo says.

"You're not wearing your yukata any more", I remark.

"You expect me to cook for you in a yukata?" she retorts in fluent English. I chuckle.

"Do you run this place by yourself?"

"Yes, I do. As you can probably tell, business is booming."

She's funny and beautiful. Her dimples are noticeably deep when she smiles. Her brown eyes sparkle with mischievousness.

"Well, I can probably help you with that. Do you have a menu?" I ask.

"No, we don't have menus in La Porte. What would you like to eat?"

"Oh my God! Is this like the show *Shinya Shokudo*? Can I order anything I want? Should I call you Master?"

She exaggerates her look of shock, hands covering her mouth, eyes wide open. And then we both start laughing.

"You can call me Megumi. And yes, I guess La Porte is a bit like *Shinya Shokudo*, except for the fact that I don't open at midnight."

"Yoroshiku[6] ne, Megumi-san. You can call me Kiku."

---

[5] *Irasshaimase*—"Welcome" or "Come in"

"Yoroshiku onegaishimasu, Kiku-san. So, what would you like?"

"Butter rice!"

She bursts out laughing again. Butter rice is the favourite dish of Goro-san, one of the characters in *Shinya Shokudo* (Midnight Diner), who plays songs on his guitar for the patrons of the diner, in-lieu of paying for his meals. Each episode in the show focuses on one dish and the story behind it. Butter rice is my favourite episode.

She scoops out a bowl of steaming hot rice and cuts a slab of butter on top of it. The buttery aroma opens my nostrils and I breathe in deep.

"Here you go. How are you doing now?" she asks.

"Much better than this afternoon. I think I blacked out in the museum."

"What happened? I thought you were having a seizure but your body was frozen stiff."

"I don't remember", I lie. I recall the screaming blue people who had sounded like cicadas.

I recall the flapping of wings.

"I'm glad you're ok now. You passed out and the museum attendants took you back to your hotel. I kept my card in your wallet in case you wanted to talk about what happened. It's not uncommon for people to feel uncomfortable in the old Abashiri prison. There's a lot of history in that place. A lot of bad things happened there."

I recall their open mouths, their flaming blue orbs.

"Prisoners were routinely beaten and abused there. So many tortured souls. That prison was their final stop in life and they all knew it. Some tried to kill themselves and were punished severely for trying. Many were placed in solitary confinement. They would scream all night until they were beaten

---

[6] *Yoroshiku*—Pleased to meet you

to unconsciousness. Or sometimes to death." Megumi explains.

I hear their screams that sound like a thousand cicadas crying.

"What do you do there?" I ask, trying to change the subject.

"Oh, I don't go there often. I'm something like a part-time consultant and go there only when the museum attendants need help."

"Help with what?"

"Stuff", she smiles.

"Like tourists passing out in the afternoon?"

"Obviously. How do you think I made all this money?" she gestures to her tiny, incense smoke filled diner. "How's your butter rice?"

I look at the empty bowl in front of me and smile. I have no idea when I finished it.

"Okawari[7]?" she asks.

"Onegaishimasu[8]", I reply.

---

[7] *Okawari*—Second helping
[8] *Onegaishimasu*— Yes, please

8. Ganesh

Ganesh has always wanted to see that light again. That warm blue colour. He's crying now as he tries to remember. Or maybe he's crying because it's taking forever to saw through Mr. Gupta's leg. God damn Mr. Gupta. His fat disgusting leg is oozing blood and fats all over the plastic tarp. Even in death he gives Ganesh grief.

Mr. Gupta was an English teacher in one of the best English medium schools in Nagpur. He lived alone. In his spare time, he gave English coaching to the high school children in the neighbourhood. Lord knows that teaching is a trying profession because Mr. Gupta liked to take the stress of educating young minds out on the stray dogs running amok in the streets of Nagpur. He also liked to cook, although mutton curry was literally the only thing Ganesh had ever seen him make. He made it in large batches. Enough to feed himself for a week and a little extra to add the Pentobarbital in. This Pentobarbital laced mutton was stored lovingly in tiffin boxes for the dogs. And honestly, which starving street dog wouldn't happily gobble up some mutton curry from a benevolent stranger, Pentobarbital laced or not. Once the dog (or sometimes, a group of dogs) was out cold, Mr. Gupta would come back in his Maruti van, wrap the dog up in a blanket and transport it back to his farmhouse a few kilometres outside the city where the killing could commence. No one misses street dogs. Or even when people do, they assume the worst and soon forget. Such is life.

His farmhouse is quite modest but impressive in utility for its small size. There's air-conditioning, cable television, a small kitchen with lots of imported canned food, a small bedroom with a queen-sized mattress, a small television with a DVD player and some pornographic DVDs. Just next to it is a tiny barn that has surgical instruments, hammers, saws, restraints, a meat grinder, a variety of chemicals and surgical tables with drains in place for all the blood. Ganesh had to bring very little of his own equipment this time; only some plastic tarp and his trusty bowie knife. And this may have been a mistake because his own hacksaw would've done a way better job of cutting through human bone. Mr. Gupta's tiny hacksaw was more suitable for dogs. But it's a bit too late for that now. He's been hacking away for hours and he's only been able to make it halfway through the body of Mr. Gupta. Ganesh planned to use almost the same methods Mr. Gupta employed on the dogs—

First, he restrains the dogs on the surgical tables.

Second, he cuts them open and slowly disembowels them while keeping them awake and howling in pain.

Third, he crushes their head with his bare hands. Ganesh opted to drive his bowie knife through Mr. Gupta's heart while Mr. Gupta sobbed and kept asking "Why? Why? Why?" which soon gave way to incoherent gurgling.

Fourth, he dismembers the dogs and grinds them up into a thick pink paste using the meat grinder—skin, bones and everything.

And finally, he takes this dog paste in a large freezer bag to the countryside to feed the stray dogs there. Circle of life.

Ganesh is on the first part of step four and Mr. Gupta's large body isn't helping.

He's been observing Mr. Gupta for months now. Mr. Gupta is calm, methodical and almost benevolent in the way he approaches the process of killing. As much as Ganesh hates to admit it, he has learned much from Mr. Gupta on his spirit walks. Fortunately for Ganesh, most of Mr. Gupta's murdering is carried out at night. It's also the time Ganesh can release his spirit from his body to spy on him.

This whole spirit walking business started long before Mr. Gupta appeared on Ganesh's 'spirit radar'. The first time it happened was five years ago, when he fell asleep on his left arm and woke up to find it hovering above him while his physical arm lay dead underneath his head. At first, he panicked and started rubbing his arm vigorously to help recirculate the blood. It was a strange feeling, as Ganesh's spirit arm and physical arm merged together. The second time was a month after that when he woke up to see him looking at himself. His spirit was outside while his body lay there like a husk. After that night, his out-of-body experiences became increasingly frequent.

He thought nothing more of them than dreams at first. But it soon became apparent that there was something very different about them. He listed down the differences—

First, he felt more awake during his spirit walks than he did during his other dreams.

Second, he could move his spirit of his own volition unlike dreams where he had no control. He could fly and pass through objects with ease.

Third, he could gather information about his surroundings that he otherwise would not have known through a dream. For example—what time his father came home at night. Or where he parked his car. Or where the local paan wala[9] kept the extra money he wanted to hide from his wife.

A few months after that, his spirit started finding people who were up to something slightly darker. It was attracted to the darkness. The first time he took notice of something strange was when he came across Mr. Tripathi. Mr. Tripathi was giving a five-star candy bar to a street urchin and patting the matted hair on her small head. Ganesh noticed the dried blood on the inside of her leg. She was crying while he consoled her, "Don't tell anyone what happened. We just played a little game. Now take your chocolate. Don't tell anyone or I will beat you. Isn't that right?"

Ganesh's spirit had this instant urge to put a knife through him. But you can't touch or interact with anything while you're a spirit. You're immaterial. All you can do is watch. And so, he did. For the next four weeks he watched Mr. Tripathi lure street kids into his car, rape them, sometimes beat them and then leave them with a five-star candy bar and a pat on the head.

Ganesh's hatred for him grew stronger with each passing day. In the

---

[9] *Paan wala*—A vendor who sells paan, a popular Indian dish made from betel leaves, areca nut and tobacco

daytime, during college lectures, he would make notes about his observations from the night before. Where Mr. Tripathi lived, how many people lived with him (he lived with his wife and two children), what time and how often he would make his candy-bar runs (every Friday night around 21:00), where he kept his car keys, how many entrances there were to his home. Before he knew it, Ganesh was already planning to murder him. It was the right thing to do. How could such a man be allowed to live? Surely this gift was given to him for a purpose? Who else could put a stop to this? Who else could bring justice? Street urchins are like street dogs in India; whether one lives, dies or disappears is nobody's business. They are the orphans of society. If he were to report Mr. Tripathi, he'd probably be put in jail for a few days or maybe not even that. What proof would he have? The word of a street urchin and a spirit walking lunatic? What good is a voice that cannot be heard?

He had to do something. He could feel it. He needed to kill Tripathi.

One of Mr. Tripathi's rituals after a candy-bar run was to visit a local dhaba[10] to eat some meat and drink a few beers. His family was vegetarian, so Ganesh supposed he liked to indulge in all the things he craved for in a single night; living flesh, dead flesh and spirit. He told his wife that he had a weekly business meeting that ran late every Friday. And off he'd go. On one such Friday night, Ganesh was waiting for him at his favourite dhaba. While he gorged himself on Tandoori chicken and Kingfisher beer, Ganesh watched Mr. Tripathi quietly from a table nearby. After Tripathi finished, he went to the toilet to wash his hands. Ganesh made his way to his own car and parked behind Mr. Tripathi's car.

Rag—check.

Chloroform—check.

Bowie knife—check.

Heavy duty cable ties—check.

---

[10] *Dhaba*—Roadside restaurant in India

Smelling salts—check.

Plastic tarp—check.

Full body raincoat—check.

Chloroform soaked rag in hand, he waited for Mr. Tripathi in the bushes next to his car. This was actually happening, he remembered thinking to himself. Adrenaline and excitement coursed through his body. He had to close his eyes and calm his hurried breathing. His senses were razor-sharp. He felt as if a completely different part of him was waking up from a deep slumber. He heard footsteps crunching through the gravel. He heard the keys jangling in Mr. Tripathi's pocket as he took them out. Ganesh stepped out of the bushes. Before he knew what was happening, Mr. Tripathi's eyes were rolling back in their sockets as he had the rag forced into his face. He was a small man and there was hardly any trouble for Ganesh to subdue him. He looked around to see if anyone had seen them. Nobody. He dragged Mr. Tripathi's limp body into the rear seat of his car. He tied his hands behind his back and his ankles together using cable ties.

Ganesh drove to an abandoned construction site that he had scouted a week earlier. He parked his car and took a brief stroll to see if there was anyone else there. It was just them. Mr. Tripathi and him. He laid out the plastic tarp on the ground and changed into his raincoat. He then dragged Mr. Tripathi out of the car and onto the tarp. Mr. Tripathi woke up trembling from the smelling salts that Ganesh waved under Mr. Tripathi's nose.

"Who…wha….wha…where am I?"

"Shhhhh…it's ok. It's ok."

"Who…who are you? Where am I?"

"I've been watching you Mr. Tripathi."

"Wha…do I know you? Who are you?"

"I've seen what you do to the children, Mr. Tripathi. Tell me, did you have fun with any children tonight?"

Mr. Tripathi's face grew pale. His eyes were wide as he stared into Ganesh's.

"I am making my stand", whispered Ganesh.

Ganesh raised the knife high above his head with both hands. Moonlight glinted on its sharp blade. Ganesh plunged it deep into Mr. Tripathi's chest.

Tripathi gasped.

As the lights went out from Mr. Tripathi's eyes, Ganesh saw something else there. Something strange. Something blue. A warm blue flame, glowing bright in his eyes. It was beautiful. As Mr. Tripathi stopped breathing, so did Ganesh, mesmerized by its glow. What was it? Was it his soul being reflected in Mr. Tripathi's dead eyes? It felt so familiar, yet so foreign. In that moment Ganesh felt as if there were two of him. And the two together made him whole. The feeling only lasted for a moment but it has stayed with him ever since that night five years ago.

He didn't see the flame in Mr. Gupta's eyes. He didn't see it in the eyes of the nine other people between him and Mr. Tripathi. Why? Why only the first time? There must be a reason. He ponders these questions as he saws through Mr. Gupta's neck. Always saw the best for last. You'll make a fine meal for the neighbourhood dogs, won't you Mr. Gupta?

9. Ame

I lost track of how long Megumi and I talked last night. I ate four bowls of butter rice and sampled some locally brewed beer which was surprisingly good. Actually, it shouldn't come as a surprise because everything in Hokkaido has tasted amazing so far. She made yakisoba for herself. We talked about Japan, Singapore, my travels, TV shows and music. She loves math rock and classical music, just like me. She had portable Bluetooth speakers which we used to play songs from each other's music libraries. We played Chopin, Toe, Uchuu Conbeni, Foo Fighters, Yoko Kanno, Debussy, The Shins, Ikue Asazaki, a mish-mash of classical, rock, indie and folk. There weren't any other customers except for me last night and I was thankful for it. Eventually, my phone's battery ran out and her charger couldn't charge my phone. She wrote her number down on her business card for me.

Don't get too excited. She's just being polite, said Jojo.

She asked me if I wanted to go and visit Shari with her on the weekend. I had no idea where Shari was and agreed to go without a second thought.

We're on a train from Abashiri to Shiretokoshari now. We don't talk much and quietly enjoy the beautiful scenery. I'm nervous and excited at the same time. To our left is the Sea of Okhotsk and to our right are the mountains. The sea crashes gently on the northern banks of Hokkaido. The sky is a beautiful shade of blue. Large cotton-candy clouds cast their shadows on azure waters. They help to calm my nerves.

We change to a bus at Shiretokoshari and continue our journey to Shiretoko. On the bus, a few seats away from us, is a blue person. His blue flame is distracting and I try my best to ignore his existence. Megumi falls asleep to the gentle rocking of the bus as it weaves through the mountainous roads. Her head leans on my shoulder and she breathes quietly through her nose, her breasts rising and falling inside her denim jacket.

We alight at Utoro in Shiretoko. The blue person continues his journey to god knows where. I take a deep breath of the fresh air that surrounds me and stretch my body. Shiretoko is a gorgeous town. There are snow-capped mountains in the distance and the sea to the north. Just like Abashiri, drift ice floats from Russia to Shiretoko in the winters and the sea looks as if it's frozen over. At least in the photos it does. East of Shiretoko is nothing but beautiful wilderness.

Megumi and I spend the morning walking the boardwalks of one of the beautiful Goko lakes. There are five lakes in total and they are supposed to represent the fingerprints of god. Megumi warns me to keep talking as we walk because the area is notorious for bear sightings and it's always a good idea to keep making sounds so that the bears are aware of your presence. Some backpackers attach tiny bells to their backpacks. Bears tend to stay away from human beings, unless they're really hungry or if they've been fed by irresponsible tourists in the past.

Talking is definitely not a problem for us. I enjoy talking to Megumi. She asks me more about my work and Singapore. She makes fun of my Singlish turrets.

"Liddat lor!" she would laugh, imitating me. I mostly blush when she does that.

I tell her that I used to live in India but converted to a Singapore citizenship a few years back. In true Singaporean fashion, I compliment the weather of Hokkaido and complain about the perpetually hot and humid weather of Singapore in the same breath. We talk more about TV shows and movies. She's a huge fan of Studio Ghibli movies, just like me, and we lament over the retirement of one of the founders of the studio, Hayao Miyazaki-san. His movies are full of nostalgia and heart. The thing I like the most about his films is that he always creates strong female leads who do not need a man to come and save them. They live life on their own terms and they live a life of courage; qualities that I feel are severely missing from my own life.

"Does your family live in Singapore too?" Megumi asks.

"My foster father still lives in India. My mother passed away when I was young and I was put in an orphanage for a short time. I don't remember much from that time at all. I left home when I was fifteen to study in Singapore. My father and I aren't that close and I rarely go back to India these days. The last time I saw him must've been more than four years ago. What about your family?"

"I'm an orphan too", Megumi replies.

"Do you have any foster parents?"

Megumi hesitates. "Sort of. It's complicated."

I decide not to probe further because I can see that it might be a sensitive subject for her. The wind picks up and is slightly colder than before. We hear rumbling in the distance. We board the bus back to Utoro just in time, before it starts pouring. The heavens open up to let loose a torrent of rain. The skies swiftly change colour from blue to dark grey. Rain water coats the bus windows and moves like honey on a piece of toast. The rain is so heavy that the bus driver decides to stop at the side of the road to let it die down. Loud cracks of thunder elicit screams and laughter from the passengers. Megumi is silent.

"It's like a proper storm", I say, trying to start a conversation with her.

Megumi says nothing.

Stop being such a needy little bitch and leave her alone, complains Jojo.

I'm not being needy. Or am I? Needy for what exactly? I feel a familiar heavy numbness in my chest; my default state.

"What do you call rain in Japanese?"

"Ame", Megumi flatly replies without looking at me. She's seated at the window seat, preferring to look at the storm outside.

Ame batters the roof of our bus. It falls in sheets, rhythmically. The sea foams and roils in the distance. Strong winds skim billows of mist off its surface. I wish I could open the windows and let the storm in.

"I waited for her", Megumi says and then pauses for a while. I sit quietly.

"That's the earliest memory I have of my mother. Waiting on the porch of a forgotten home while it rained outside. I waited for her. I don't even remember her face but I remember the waiting. I waited for two days while it rained relentlessly. I remember eating bugs from the floor because there was no one to feed me. I cried and waited and cried and waited. She never came back."

"How old were you?" I ask.

"Maybe two or three."

"Who saved you in the end?"

"Old Jiji, my foster father, saved me. He came through the rain and took me with him. I think I left a part of me inside that house that day. Crying and waiting, crying and waiting. But of course, you never leave anything behind. You carry everything with you. Somewhere inside me, it's still raining."

"Sometimes it's better to forget", I say.

Megumi turns to face me and shakes her head in disagreement.

"My home is empty

It waits for me to return

Even when I'm there"

I count the syllables in my head. It's a haiku.

"I don't understand what it means", I admit.

"Your heart knows what it means", she insists.

"Like fuck, it does", I snort dismissively.

My disbelief obviously doesn't please Megumi as her face twists into a scowl. What? My numb heart knows what her haiku means? I don't like riddles. I prefer people to be straightforward with me instead of going around in circles. She turns to face the rain again.

The rain lets up after a while, just enough for the bus driver to make it back to Utoro, wet and moody passengers in tow. We change to a bus that takes us back to Shiretokoshari. We don't exchange a single word all this time, sitting next to each other, one person sulking and the other annoyed.

I finally break the silence by saying, "I'm sorry".

"Why are you sorry?"

"For being rude earlier", I explain.

"You don't understand what I'm upset about so there's no point in apologizing to me", Megumi tells me.

Aiyah, just accept the apology lah. Why must we make everything so convoluted?

"Fine then. What are you upset about?"

"It doesn't matter, Kiku. You wouldn't get it. I feel your heart is closed right now."

I have nothing else to say to her. I busy myself in the task of buying train tickets back to Abashiri. The next train is an hour away. Great. Now I have to sit here with a sulking girl I barely know who likes to speak in riddles. I walk around the train station to find some snacks and drinks to buy. I decide to buy an extra can of green tea for Megumi as a peace offering. I go and place the can next to her seat and walk away without looking back. It's still raining outside when I go out for a smoke. I didn't bring my pack of cigarettes with me. How odd, I had completely forgotten about smoking the whole day until just now.

It's cold and wet. Just the kind of weather I like. I keep expecting Megumi to come and join me outside, maybe thank me for the drink and talk to me.

See, you're a needy little bitch after all, says Jojo.

The train arrives. Megumi chooses not to sit with me and sits a few seats away. I wonder if I should go and sit with her or just give her some space. This whole day is falling apart, isn't it? After we get down at Abashiri, I will probably never see her again. That's what always happens. That's why I can't trust anyone. Everyone leaves.

You won't leave me like they did, will you? You won't go away now will you?

Whose voice was that? That wasn't Jojo. That was someone else. I feel a chill inside me. I wipe my face and find that there's sweat on it. My right hand is clenching and unclenching by itself. I grab it hard to stop its involuntary motions. I look around to see if there are any blue people nearby but there's no one. The train leaves the station and plunges itself into the rain.

Ame, Megumi had said. Her mother had abandoned her and someone else took her in. Just like me. I'm surprised that she has such young memories of her childhood. I hardly remember anything from before the age of ten. I don't even remember who my friends were at that age. Did I even have any friends? There was a boy at the orphanage long ago but I can't remember his name. I start feeling sleepy every time I try to remember the past. The rain keeps falling rhythmically on the train window. The scenes outside blur in and out of my vision like a water painting someone poured water on, the colours running off the edges. Before I know it, I'm lost to sleep.

10. Family Portrait

I am lying naked on the cold floor. There's a storm brewing outside. There is no sunlight pouring through the leaves outside into the dark room. There are only clouds. Dark blue light streams through the windows from a lighthouse and casts shadows on a family of three—a mother, a father and a son. They're smiling for a family portrait. None of them have eyes, only hollow sockets. I don't have my camera with me. Where's the camera, I ask them. They grin a manic grin. A crow lands on the boy's shoulder. I look at the crow, the crow looks at me.

"I will eat you", the crow says.

"Like fuck you will", I say.

The crow flies out of the window and towards the lighthouse. The father takes out a knife and slits the boy's throat. He then slit's the mother's throat.

He looks at me and sobs, "You looked inside! You looked inside me! You won't leave me like they did, will you? You won't go away now will you?"

The father slits his own throat.

Their black blood pools on the floor and creeps towards me. I can't move. I don't want their blood to touch me. It's going to be cold and sticky. Cold. Sticky. Cold and sticky. The blood touches my right hand, making it cold and sticky. I clench and unclench my cold and sticky right hand.

Clench and unclench.

Clench and unclench.

A dark shadow falls on me. I look up and see a giant crow-man—large, black and terrifying. Its black wings shimmer in the blue light. Its liquid eyes ooze out blackness. The crow-man looks at me quizzically, its head tilting from side to side.

"You got away", it says and closes in to peck me.

11. Oyakodon

"NO", I shout.

We are about to reach Abashiri, the announcement on the train says. There's a concerned old lady sitting next to me who offers me her tea. I politely decline. Did I just shout in my sleep? I rub my eyes and stand up to see where Megumi is seated. Good, she's still there. I walk out and sit next to her.

"Hi", I say.

"Hi", she replies.

"I had a bad dream", I tell her.

"What did you see?"

"I saw a crow trying to eat me."

Megumi scrunches up her thin eyebrows, "where were you in the dream?"

"I don't remember. There was a lighthouse somewhere, I think."

"Have you ever been to a lighthouse before?"

"Not that I can recall. I may have as a child but I doubt it. The place where I used to live in India is far away from the sea."

"What did the lighthouse look like in your dream?"

"I don't remember."

"What about the crow?"

"It was huge", I say, "almost like a man."

"Did the crow say anything to you?"

"I think it did, but I forgot what it said."

I rub my eyes. And then my chest. The heavy numbness in my chest is back again. We alight at Abashiri station. Megumi grabs my hand and says, "Let's go get something to eat."

"Where do you want to go?" I ask, fully aware of the touch of her hand but pretending I don't notice.

"I'll make us some oyakodon. We can go and get some chicken from the supermarket. I have the rest of the ingredients at home."

"Sure, oyakodon sounds good."

Both our stomachs rumble in agreement before we break out in hysterical laughter. I feel the heaviness in me melt a bit.

Megumi picks a supermarket close to her home. In spite of my terrible sense of direction, I recognize the streets that I had been walking up and down a few nights before, searching for La Porte. She buys chicken and cigarettes. I buy a small susuwatari[11] charm for her because she told me they're extremely cute when we were talking about Studio Ghibli movies. She can't stop giggling when I give it to her on the way to her apartment. She thanks me and kisses me on the cheek.

Be careful, warns Jojo.

Her apartment is on the seventh floor of another derelict building in the same neighbourhood. I'm starting to wonder if there are any new buildings in Abashiri or if everything here was built in the 1950s. While we wait for the elevator, she holds my hand again. We look at each other briefly and then we kiss. Her hair smells of mint leaves. It makes my head feel light. I kiss her again, softly this time and then with a feverish intensity as we enter the elevator. She manages to press the seventh floor button as she laughs at my enthusiasm. I must've been too rough because I feel her push me away

---

[11] *Susuwatari*—Susuwatari or soot sprites (conjured from soot itself) are small, black, fuzzy creatures with spherical bodies and white eyes with black pupils. They make an appearance in Studio Ghibli anime movies such like Totoro and Spirited Away

a bit before we both relax and enjoy the feeling of each other's lips.

Just like her restaurant, her apartment is right at the end of the corridor, facing the elevator. She holds my hand and leads me towards it. I feel nervous. When was the last time I had sex? I had a girlfriend in college and I've never been the type to hook up with strangers. How long ago was that? Ten years ago? I was always high on my meds back then and that entire time feels like a foggy dream to me. Megumi squeezes my hand, as if to tell me it's fine. I try my best to act normal and relaxed even though my insides are in turmoil. Before I enter her apartment, she stops me.

"I sense that there are two of you. I would like to know if the other means me any harm."

"What?"

Are there two of us? Jojo asks.

None of us answers the other's question. Eyes closed, Megumi hovers her hand over my chest for a silent minute. I find myself looking at the ceiling and the walls around us. After a minute, she opens her eyes and smiles a satisfied smile, dimples showing.

"You have my permission to enter."

Something inside me feels warm as I walk through the door.

12. My Heart Will Go On

Ganesh has been travelling farther and farther on his spirit walks lately. He realized that he can launch his spirit out of his body at great speeds to cover great distances. Like a soul catapult. On good nights, he can jump all the way up to the sky where the birds fly. Just a little higher and he can reach the clouds. The feeling is liberating. Everything looks smaller from up there. The ground below looks like a spider's web, woven out of yellow light.

This feeling of liberation worries him because he doesn't feel like returning when the sun comes up. He has slept through his alarms the last few times. In his head he can hear the alarm ringing, but he chooses to fly for an extra minute or so which sometimes turns into a few hours. What if he were to fly away forever and never return? Would that be so bad? His body would react violently at the thought and bring him back whenever that happens.

Other strange things have been happening too. Ganesh has started sleeping earlier and earlier and he goes on spirit walks even before the sun sets. On some of his flights, he finds himself in the homes of families. Ordinary families. Going about their mundane existence. Watching TV, eating dinner, grunting and snorting while passionlessly coupling. Ganesh would hang around in their homes and merely observe. He didn't think much of it at first and would just let his mind wander for a while before getting bored and flying off. But soon, he realized that he was visiting the same families over and over again. Why? These aren't dog murderers or pedophiles. Nothing about these people seems out of place. What's even weirder is that he finds himself absentmindedly scribbling addresses and times in his notebook while he's awake.

Malhotra family, 4 members—4 Saibaba Nagar, Flat 404—
16:55—Rahul and Shweta come home after school
18:00—Rahul goes for math tuition
18:30—Shweta goes for singing lessons

18:30—only mother is at home
18:45—milkman delivery
19:00—best time to hide
19:30—Rahul comes home from tuition
19:40—father comes home from work
19:50—Shweta comes home from lessons
21:00—everyone has dinner together
22:00—everyone goes to sleep
23:00— :)

Why did I draw the smiley face, he wonders? And "best time to hide"? Hide from what? In their home? What for?

He's been buying a lot of sewing supplies too. Nothing fancy. Nylon threads, needles of all sizes, heavy cloth scissors—the kind you can cut off a person's fingers with. Why he's buying them, he has no idea. He just feels the urge to buy them and so he does. People often do things without giving them a second thought. As if their body has a mind of its own.

And just like that, absentmindedly, Ganesh finds himself in the Malhotras' home one night. I'm here again, he groans to himself, annoyed. He doesn't notice his own shadow at first. Or the gloves. Or the raincoat. Or the sewing kit that he's carrying with him. This is odd, he thinks. Am I carrying objects? His hand tries to pass through the walls but it doesn't. He pokes and prods the wall a few more times. Very odd indeed.

Ganesh is suddenly aware that his physical body has decided to tag along on his spirit walk. In fact, this isn't a spirit walk at all. He's here. In person. With gloves on and a sewing kit in hand.

He carefully places the plastic sewing kit on the floor and unclips it. Inside he finds, neatly arranged, his bowie knife, several spools of nylon thread, a variety of large threading needles and what appears to be a skinning knife. As quiet as a mouse, Ganesh clips back the sewing kit and sees himself out of the front door. He takes his raincoat and gloves off and walks downstairs. He's in a strange building, yet he knows where to go. He has scouted this place thoroughly without his own knowledge. On the ground floor is the parking lot. He didn't bring his car. Of course not. He was planning to murder this family. And stitch them together, or something to that effect. He's sweating profusely now as he briskly exits the building. He doesn't even know where he is. Oh right, he's at 4 Saibaba Nagar, like he had written down earlier. It's 23:11 on his watch. Did he already murder the Malhotra family? He stops at the corner and looks around to see if anyone has noticed him. There are people on the streets, even at this time. It's best to just keep walking. It takes him half an hour to get home. He quietly slips in and goes up to his room on the second floor of the landed house. The first thing he does is to open the sewing kit again to check both the knives for blood. Nothing. He smells them too for good measure. Next, he strips his clothes and puts them into a plastic bag, along with the raincoat, to burn them later. He takes a long hot shower to scrub his skin properly. Sleep comes as soon as his head hits the pillow.

That night Ganesh goes farther than he's ever gone before. He flies for hours and hours, trying to get as far away as possible from his body. He can feel something tugging and pulling inside him, like he is trying to rip himself in two. Since when has he started spying on innocent families? What the hell was he doing with all that equipment in their home? He has always punished those who are wrong. Those who have done wrong to the world. Those who prey on the weak. Those who deserve it. What has this family of four done to deserve his brand of justice?

Ganesh is suddenly aware that he's not flying in the sky any more. He sees trees zipping past him, through him. He's inside a forest. Something about the forest feels familiar and foreign at the same time. He slows down and eventually decides to land. His feet touch the forest floor. That's strange, he usually doesn't feel the ground. Is he here in person again? The thought only troubles him for a moment. Maybe he's dreaming. And that's fine, because he hasn't dreamt in a long time. He walks on the soft grass and leaves. With each step he feels heavier, more whole. He walks on and on, through the dense forest. Minutes pass, maybe hours. He can hear a woman singing somewhere far away. Her beautiful melody fills the forest and makes the leaves sway in tune. Hasn't he heard this song before? The song says to him, "go on and on…"

Ganesh notices there's something on his ears. Something plastic and circular. They're headphones. Blue headphones. He can hear the song more clearly now.

"Love was when I loved you,

One true time I hold to…"

In front of him is an overturned bus, laying on its side. The front of the bus has collapsed in on itself. The rear wheels sticking up in the air are still turning. The mangled mass of steel seems out of place in the forest, yet it feels like it's exactly where it's supposed to be. A crow sits on top of the bus, looking at him inquisitively.

"Near, far, wherever you are…"

Somewhere far away, an alarm goes off.

There's something inside the bus. Something Ganesh needs to see. He steps closer to the bus which isn't overturned any more. The windows are shattered. Blood streaks mark the sides of the bus in parallel lines. The doors of the bus are bent into a K shape.

"Once more, you open the door…"

Ganesh's body rebels, his hands start shaking violently. Come back, his body is screaming to him. But he must see what's inside. He needs to see. His hands are on the bus doors. He feels the crook of the K under his fingertips. He traces his fingers along the bent metal until he reaches the mangled door handle, his hands trembling all the way.

He starts pulling.

His body starts pulling him back.

The alarm grows louder.

The song grows louder too.

"You're here, there's nothing I fear…"

The door starts to give away. I must keep pulling, he screams to himself.

Come back, he hears his body scream.

The door comes off its hinges and Ganesh falls back with the door in his hands. He throws the door aside, picks himself up and rushes inside the bus.

Inside the bus is a cold dark night. There's a man laid out on a plastic tarp. Another larger man, wearing a raincoat, is on top of him. The larger man is holding a bowie knife above his head, ready to plunge it in. He has no face and a flaming blue orb on top of him. It's a beautiful, mesmerizing blue.

"Watch as I teach you", the faceless man says.

Moonlight glints on the sharp blade of the knife.

Just then, Ganesh falls off the bed.

He's back in his bedroom, tangled up in the bedsheets and drenched in sweat. His body is aching. The alarm keeps on ringing and ringing and ringing.

13. The White Bathroom

We lie in bed, holding each other. My breath is coming through my nostrils, shrilly and trembling. For the first time in a long time, my shoulders aren't feeling tense like they usually do. I feel free.

"I think I really like you", I say.

Megumi's face contorts into a smirk. It's only for a moment, before she bursts into laughter. She's laughing at me. Of course, she is. I look away from her face and at the rest of her naked body, trying to absorb the image in my mind. But I keep hitting a wall. I can feel my face contorting too, my forehead tensed and wrinkly. From the corner of my eye I see her hand move away from under her head where it had been resting.

She touches me.

"How can you like someone else when you can't love yourself?" she asks gently.

I can feel the tightness in my chest concentrate into a small ball. Is this a riddle too? *She pities us,* Jojo points out. I start to grit my teeth slowly, incisors on incisors. The top incisors scrape over the bottom row and the bottom scrape under the top. Back and forth, back and forth, back and forth. The ball of tightness pulses inside my chest in tune with the scraping. I stare blankly at her mouth, my eyes darting to meet her cold brown eyes and then back to her mouth. I should say something.

"I'm sorry, I didn't mean it", I manage to blurt out an apology.

"Oh? I thought you liked me?" she laughs.

I roll my eyes and look away. How funny indeed—saying that I like someone I barely know.

She picks up a bottle of mineral water from her dresser, takes a sip and offers it to me. I realize that my throat has gone dry. As I drink from the bottle, I'm more aware of my nakedness and the coldness of the semen still wrapped around my shrunken penis inside the condom.

"Want to go outside for a smoke?" she asks as she gets out of bed to slip on her black t-shirt and a pair of black panties.

I welcome the break from the post-proposal awkwardness. "Sure", I say before going to the bathroom to clean up.

I have a bad habit of snooping on other people when I'm in their homes. Looking into their medicine cabinets, looking for any clues on what makes them who they are. Megumi's bathroom though is like something out of a science fiction movie. Actually, it's more like what you would expect to see in a prison if prisons had private bathrooms. Everything is white. The floor and walls are covered in white tiles with a metal railing for her white towel. There's a bar of white soap on a tray below the shower, a large mirror on top of a large white sink, a white mug for her toothbrush and toothpaste, both white. There's shampoo and conditioner on the sink (both white bottles too) and underneath the sink is a tiny white dustbin. The tiny garbage bag inside the tiny white dustbin, thankfully, is black. Tucked away in the corner is a white commode with a roll of white toilet paper on top of the white flush tank. There are no curtains. Or colours. There's no medicine cabinet hiding behind the mirror. There aren't any candles or tubs or beauty products. Everything about her bathroom screams functional.

Look, she's dead inside, just like you! Jojo laughs. I let out a stifled chuckle as I finish cleaning up and grab her white and only towel.

Megumi is already on her balcony, smoking. She looks like a vision, surrounded by the smoke and bathed in moonlight. I didn't even realize it was a full moon tonight until just now. She's smoking reds from an unfamiliar pack.

"Cabin Roast", I announce as I take a closer look at the maroon pack.

"They're amazing. どうぞ[12]", she offers.

They indeed are great. Strong and smooth, with an aftertaste of coffee. I let myself decompress and exhale a long puff. Megumi smiles at me. I smile back nervously and quickly look away from her. The balcony is very cold and the fact that I only have a towel on isn't helping. As I rub my arms and let my eyes wander to the building across the street, I see the hint of a blue flame inside one of the apartments. I squint my eyes to take a closer look but all I can see is a blue flaming ball. Just one.

"See anything?" she asks as she looks straight at the window I'm looking through.

"べつに[13]", I reply.

"That's a shame", she sighs.

"Why is it a shame?"

"I just thought you saw something", she says.

"And suppose I did?"

She turns to me and asks me in a less playful tone, "What do you see, Kiku?"

I'm slightly taken aback by her sudden seriousness. I smirk and raise my eyebrows. "Ghosts."

"Describe them."

"I don't see anything lah. Sometimes I see things that aren't there."

"Ok, then just describe what you see that isn't there!"

What's up with her? Does she see something too? I pause for a moment and scan her face. She's fully present, looking at me with an intensity I haven't seen before.

---

[12] どうぞ*(Douzo)*—Please help yourself
[13] べつに*(Betsuni)*—Nothing in particular

"I sometimes see blue orbs. Like flaming blue orbs, on top of people's heads. Except they aren't people, they're ghosts. Or maybe just figments of my imagination. They lack any colour. Like black and white photographs."

"Since when?" she asks me.

"I don't know. What do you mean by since when?"

"Since when do you see these people with blue flaming orbs?" she asks with more urgency.

She can see them too, can't she? I feel frissons all over my chest and face.

"I really don't know since when. My childhood memories are so hazy and unreliable. It's as if a thick fog has seeped into that part of my brain and only bits and pieces are able to surface from it when I try really hard. But that's what they are—bits and pieces. Flashes from a camera, scenes frozen in time. A forest with trees and yellowing grass. People on a railway platform. Or even just darkness that's dark blue."

"A forest…"

"Yeah. Anyway, what I'm trying to say is that I don't remember when I first saw them. Maybe when I was five? My doctor thinks I'm crazy." I hesitate, "Can you see them too?"

She smiles a sad smile at me. Like there's a river inside her that wants to flow out at this very moment. It beats violently at the banks of her mind but her dam is too tall for anything to spill over.

"Yes, I see them", she replies.

"What are they? Are they real?"

"They are as real as the rain that does not fall.

They live, yet they are not alive.

They seek the way because they are lost.

And in the darkness I am their guide."

We stare at each other without saying a word. Blood gushes through my heart. It traverses my arteries to my extremities and then flows back inwards, pulsing and spreading. I am aware of the sound of my beating heart. My body buzzes with all the latent energy that is inside me.

I see her. She sees me.

The moment stretches on for minutes in my head. And then it passes. I draw in a deep breath and let it out, trying to recapture the feeling. But it is gone. I am shirtless and cold on the balcony of a girl I barely know. Someone replaced the cigarette in my hand with ashes attached to a cylindrical filter.

"And in the darkness I am their guide", I repeat softly to myself.

"And in the darkness I am their guide", she replies.

"What are they?"

"They are Aoirei. 'Aoi' means blue and 'rei' means spirit. Blue spirits. And I am their guide."

"Aoirei", I repeat.

"Aoirei", she repeats.

"And you are their guide."

"I am their guide."

"What are they searching for?" I ask.

"What they search for is something only they know. I cannot find it for them, but I can show them the way if they truly want it. That's why I am their guide. You see, everyone wants to find the truth, in one form or another. We are all searching for it, whether we consciously realize it or not. Even after we die.

You and me. The Aoirei. Everyone."

She grimaces momentarily at the last part and then corrects herself, "Almost everyone."

Maybe you're the exception, Jojo says.

"So, the Aoirei are searching for the truth. What is the truth? The truth about how they became spirits? The truth about their lives?"

"The truth", she replies.

I scratch my head. She's speaking in riddles again and I'd rather not get into a philosophical debate with her. I direct my attention towards the window in the other building.

"Do you see that?" I point. "Do you see the blue flame in the window?"

"It's not *in* the window."

"Yeah lah, you know what I mean. Do you see the blue flame or not?"

"Yes, I see him."

"What is "he"?"

"That's Nakamura-san. He killed himself in that apartment and has been trying to find a way out."

"You've spoken to him?" I ask.

"Yes, several times. But he doesn't remember. He always forgets."

"Why did he kill himself?"

"Well…" Megumi pauses, "let me get something."

She rushes into her apartment and starts rifling through the drawers. I decide to step in too to put a t-shirt on. She brings to me a large black binder and flips to one of the sleeves inside. "Here!" she proclaims and shows me an old newspaper clipping. There's an article in Japanese with an accompanying photo of a gaunt old man, hollow sunken eyes and sunken cheeks, white hair and white eyebrows. The photograph is in the centre of the article with kanji on both sides of it.

She turns the binder to herself and without me having to ask, she translates the article aloud.

"*Grandfather Kills Granddaughter and Commits Suicide*

Abashiri, February 20—Neighbours complained of the smell coming from 72 year old Nakamura Shigeyoshi's apartment. He had hanged himself in his kitchen, leaving behind a suicide note, say police officials.

In the note, he confessed to killing his granddaughter by mistake over an argument and burying her body near the banks of Lake Abashiri. Overcome by guilt, he decided to commit suicide.

After searching through the snow, all along the banks of the lake, police recovered the frozen body of a 5 year old girl who is believed to be Nakamura Aoi, the granddaughter of the deceased.

Nakamura-san was living alone with his granddaughter after his daughter had passed away in a tragic car accident, said neighbours."

I look at the window again and see the gaunt face of a lonely old man, peering out. His hands are on the window pane, cupping his face as he squints to see the world outside. His breath does not fog the window.

"He forgot everything?" I ask.

"Yes. He doesn't even remember the names of his family members, let alone my conversations with him. We take our traumas with us into the afterlife. But sometimes we are too afraid to remember."

"Have you ever watched Black Mirror?" I ask.

"No. What's that?"

"It's a British TV show. There's an episode in it called 'White Christmas'. In it, there's a man who has hidden himself away in a cabin, somewhere far away in his mind. Someone else created that cabin to trap him, but I'd like to believe it was his own doing. Every day he looks outside and all he sees is snow. You see, his daughter froze to death in the snow, searching for help because he had killed her grandfather and run away. She wanted to save her grandfather. And she died trying. The man is trapped in the cabin for eternity now, repenting for his murders. He watches his daughter die in the snow, again and again and again."

"Nakamura-san only sees snow outside that window", Megumi sighs.

Tears well up in my eyes. I don't understand why. Megumi and I look at Nakamura-san's window to the world. A white world, lost to the snow of our mind.

14. Old Jiji

Old Jiji made his way through the forest. It had been raining for twenty four days now. The roads weren't built for heavy rain and horse carts frequently got stuck in the mud. Rivers expanded to twice their size and destroyed bridges in their swelling rage. Animals, birds and insects searched for higher ground. Old Jiji, however, had no intentions of following them to safety. He trudged through the deep mud, expertly using his wooden staff to gauge where to step and which parts to avoid. His mission was of utmost importance.

The crows hounded him from time to time, but they dared not come too close lest they were in a hurry to meet an untimely demise at the end of his staff.

Jiji hadn't eaten in seven days. Hunger and thirst were but minor inconveniences that only served to annoy him when he rested for a few hours every night. At night he dreamt about how young Natsu had once cried at having let a young boy die at the Karasu's black hands. Good, he thought. She understood the consequences of being careless on that day. If only Yuki had learnt too. He remembered Yuki and her blue eyes. He remembered Kazama. And the twilight hour when the world changed. Hatred entered his heart. Jiji let the hate swirl and rage like the flood infested rivers all around him. You couldn't save her, the hate said. You let her die, it accused. Then you abandoned him, it screamed. You left him in an orphanage, it rumbled. And then the hate passed.

The rain poured down relentlessly, drenching him to the bone.

As he set off again, in the morning, he saw a figure emerging through the heavy downpour. It was a woman, wearing what used to be a blue yukata, now brown with mud.

"Ojiisan[14]! Ossan! You must help me please! Please, do you have any food? My daughter is alone and hungry. We ran out of food a few days ago. She's only a few years old and I have no food or milk left to feed her with. The rains have flooded all the roads. My husband is away fighting for the Shogun. I haven't seen him in months. We are all alone and starving, my daughter and I. Please, could you please spare us some food? Everything has been washed away in the floods. Please, could you help us? She is only a few years old."

The woman kept blubbering and clutching onto Jiji's robes.

"Where is your home?"

"It's just beyond the hill behind us. I've been walking since yesterday. I could take you there. You can have anything you want. Just please, if you could spare some food for my daughter."

"What's her name?"

The woman looked confused.

"What's her name?" Jiji repeated.

"Megumi."

"Megumi", Jiji repeated.

"Please ojiisan, you…"

THWACK

The woman's head split into two. Jiji used the mud to wipe the bone and brain off his staff. He whistled to the crows who would surely come and finish off any Aoirei; should any emerge from the woman's dead body.

"Megumi", he repeated to himself. It was a fine name for his newest Guide. There was a spring in his step as he headed towards the hill and the rain drenched house beyond.

---

[14] *Ojiisan*—Grandfather or old man

Worms dance in the rain

Twisting, writhing, frolicking

Tempting hungry mouths

15. The Lighthouses of Japan

Last night Megumi dreamt about her rain drenched home. I dreamt about the lighthouse again. It was clearer in my dream this time, white walls with a white dome on top, stark against the blue sea. The lighthouse had large windows on top. There were crows perched on every inch of the lighthouse. None of them crowed. I heard a boy crying but I couldn't find him. Suddenly it started snowing, covering everything. All the crows disappeared, leaving a numbing silence in their wake. The sea froze over. Everything was white except for the blue light pouring out of the lighthouse like liquid fire.

Megumi and I are at the public library, searching for lighthouse related books. We found a book called *The Lighthouses of Japan*. While scanning through it, I had a strange thought. What if there really was a reason to why I was seeing a lighthouse in my dreams? Megumi certainly seems to think that it's significant. When I agreed to go to the library with her, my initial intention was just to spend more time with her. But the more I look through this book now, the more convinced I am that I'll actually find the lighthouse I saw. White lighthouses with a white dome on top seem to be the go-to architectural design in Japan, so we focus more on the places that experience a lot of snow, like Hokkaido and Tohoku. After searching for half an hour (which mostly involved me gazing intently at Megumi while she gazed intently at the book), she asks, "Is this the one?"

She points to one of the photographs in the book.

"Cape Chikyu", I read out aloud as I look closely at the photograph of a short white lighthouse, situated on a cliff overlooking the sea, surrounded by greenery.

"In my dream, it was covered in snow...and crows..." I reply, "But this is definitely the one I saw."

Cape Chikyu, or Cape Earth, or Chikyumisaki, is in Muroran, Hokkaido. It gets the name Cape Earth because you can see the curvature of the earth when you look out at the sea from this cape. It's located a few train stations away from the onsen[15] town of Noboribetsu, in the southern part of Hokkaido. It takes half a day to reach Muroran from Abashiri. Megumi and I book the cheapest hotel we can find to spend the night there.

"Are you sure you want to go with me?" I ask her.

"Yes, I do. You've tapped into something, Kiku. The fact that you can see the Aoirei and have dreams about crows means that you're attuned to a different plane of existence. Not everyone can see the Aoirei. In fact, only a handful of us can. Most people go through their lives completely unaware of their surroundings, never fully present. Don't get me wrong, I see that side of you too, the one that's shut itself off. The side that doesn't want to see. But there's more to you than that. I feel it."

"Like you felt there were two of me?" I joke.

"There *are* two of you. Well, to be more precise, there's someone else inside you.

But you don't need to worry about that person..." she trails off, mischievously smiling.

Jojo says to me—*Listen dude, I'm not about to start paying rent to you or anything, ok?*

"Ok", I laugh. All three of us laugh along.

"You must think I'm crazy, but I sense her in you", Megumi says.

Her? Maybe she *is* a little crazy. But then, so am I. Medically diagnosed even.

"Can you tell me more about the crows?" I ask Megumi.

The smile disappears from her face. She says nothing for a while, as if she's gathering her thoughts. Her words are slow and measured—"The

---

[15] *Onsen*—Japanese hot spring

crows, or the Karasu, are dangerous, Kiku. They are hollow inside. They have no souls, so they hunger for them."

"Souls?"

"Yes, souls. We all have one. At least one for most people."

"I don't know if I believe in that", I say.

"What do you suppose the blue flaming orb is that the Aoirei carry with them?"

I pause to think for a moment. Are the Aoirei even real to begin with? I've heard that it's possible for people to share the same delusions under special circumstances, kind of like mass hysteria. But there was nothing hysterical about last night. We both saw Nakamura-san. We both saw the flaming blue orb that Megumi claims to be his soul. Did someone else say that to me before? Surely it couldn't have been Doctor Zhao. She'd be having a fit right now if I told her about everything that has happened in Japan so far. Who was it then that told me that the blue flaming orb was their soul? My right hand feels numb and uncomfortable as I think about it.

"Where else have you seen the Aoirei before?" I ask her.

"They're everywhere. Many of them are attached to the places that were once important to them when they were alive. Some of them appear at the spot where they died; if they died in an untimely manner that is, be it by killing themselves or by being killed by someone else. Like Abashiri prison. I myself don't know how or when an Aoirei appears. Not every person that dies turns into one. Their origin is a mystery. In my experience though, it's usually the people who are incomplete, who are still searching for something. They have no name for it, but what they're searching for is the truth. Although rare, you may find some Aoirei out in the open, detached from where they lived and died. These are the ones who've realized that they're searching for something bigger than themselves. These are the ones that are easier to guide to where they need to go."

"And where do they need to go?" I ask.

"I can't tell you that now, Kiku. It's a place that you must find for yourself, when you hear it calling."

"You mean like the lighthouse?"

"Maybe the lighthouse. Maybe not the lighthouse. We'll have to go and see what's there."

In the evening, Megumi and I pack our bags for the early train ride tomorrow. She spends the night in my hotel room and we have sex again. I'm nervous during the sex. Last time things happened so spontaneously that I just went with them. This time, it seems more deliberate and I keep wondering if I'm doing it right or if I'm going to come soon or if it's going to be as good as the last time or if what I'm doing is wrong or if…

"What's wrong, Kiku", she asks me suddenly while I'm on top of her.

I stop to catch my breath and slowly pull out. I look for my pillow and move to lay my head down on it. What's wrong? My mind is blank. I try to think of what to say, but the words don't come easily. Then suddenly, my mouth starts moving on its own—

"This whole thing feels unreal to me. The Aoirei, the lighthouse, the crows. Even you.

I think part of me doesn't want any of this to be real because then it would be easier to deal with all the shit that would come once it ends. It would have just been a dream. A figment of my imagination for not having taken my medication. No harm done.

But then another part of me keeps saying to me—don't screw this up. This is really happening. This might be the only chance you have to really connect with someone. When was the last time you actually felt all these emotions?

You're numb all the time.

Dead inside.

Wake the fuck up, Kiku."

I'm surprised by my own frankness.

I can only see one half of Megumi's face, the other half is buried in her pillow. Tears are streaming down the one brown eye that's visible to me.

"Are you alright?" I ask her.

"I don't know if I've ever been alright", she replies and starts sobbing loudly.

I don't know what to say, so I gently stroke her hair and let her cry it out. The tears keep falling and make a large puddle on her white pillow. I keep stroking dutifully. After crying for a while, she reaches for the tissues on the desk and blows her nose. She turns the drenched side of her pillow over and plops her head on the dry side.

"I feel like I'm not supposed to be here. I mean not like here, here, in the hotel room with you, but more like here, in this time. I feel like I don't belong to this era. Like I was supposed to be somewhere else but I'm here now. I numb myself to these feelings by going about the task of guiding the Aoirei. Sometimes I find a guy to fuck and distract myself. But is this really what my life is meant to be about? When I first saw you at the prison, I thought you were cute, with your neatly parted hair and everything. I wanted to see you again, hoping that we would fuck. I didn't want anything more than that. And now that I know you can see the Aoirei too, I'm starting to look back at the kind of life I've led so far. Never connecting with anyone, always numb. Like you said about yourself—dead inside."

The tears start rolling down her eyes again but she wipes them away with efficient strokes of her hand.

"Listen Kiku, I don't know why we met, but there must be a reason for it. There has to be. I don't know what we'll find in Muroran, but I would like to go on this journey with you."

The look in her eyes tells me that she means it. I slip my arm underneath her neck to pull her close to me.

"Then let's go together", I whisper softly.

16. The Orphans

Ganesh spits blood and milk teeth out on the dormitory floor. He's gotten beatings from the other boys before but never this bad. The altercation began with a simple enough misunderstanding. Ganesh had eaten the Toblerone chocolates that someone had donated to the orphanage. By himself. The Sister had kept them out on her desk and Ganesh had stolen them. Jojo had warned him not to, but he didn't listen. The older boys didn't appreciate the fact that he hadn't shared the spoils of his thievery. And now he was getting a beating worse than he had ever gotten before.

"Eh, he's spitting blood! That's enough, we should go now before Sister sees!" one of the smaller boys says, the worry evident in his voice.

"No! This dog needs to learn who's boss!" declares the ringleader, Raju. Raju is older than all the other boys and towers over everyone in both height and a sense of entitlement. When you've been abandoned by your own family, the only way to gain back what you've lost is by taking it. Or so Raju believes.

Ganesh's face is swollen and his bottom lip is split wide open, bleeding bright red blood onto his tattered shirt. He looks around, trying to find an escape, but he's cornered. Raju and his posse of four close in on the boy who's cowering in the corner, with his arms shielding his head.

Ganesh keeps saying "I'm sorry, I'm sorry", as if his cries for mercy will save him from being beaten to unconsciousness. He breathes out bubbles of blood through the gaps where his teeth used to be.

Thwack!

One of the boys falls over screaming.

Thwack!

Raju joins the other boy on the floor, screaming and covering his ear where he got hit by the business end of a cricket bat.

"You want some more?" Jojo shouts at them, swinging a cricket bat a few sizes too large for his body.

"What's going on? What's all that noise?"

Everyone scatters when they hear the nuns shouting from the corridor outside.

Jojo hides the bat under one of the beds and grabs Ganesh's hand to pick him up. Ganesh looks at his saviour through tear stained eyes. Jojo stands thin and tall in front of him, hair neatly parted to the side as always, his hand holding Ganesh's.

"You must learn to make your stand", Jojo says to Ganesh.

A month later, Jojo was adopted by a single father and he left the orphanage forever. Ganesh never forgot Jojo. Jojo represented justice. Justice in a world that didn't care for the downtrodden. Justice in a world that turned a blind eye to the helpless. And even though a part of Ganesh died a few years later, the part of him that admired Jojo, and what he stood for, lived on inside him.

17. Promises

Megumi and I reach Muroran in the afternoon. We waste no time, leaving our luggage in the lobby of our hotel, as we head towards Chikyumisaki. It's a bright and sunny day. White clouds float sluggishly in the stark blue sky. The sun plays hide and seek with us, peeking in and out of clouds. Megumi is wearing a blue cardigan over a white t-shirt with black denim jeans. I have my black weatherproof jacket on me. She comments that I would look very sexy in a black suit. I make a mental note of it.

The walk to Chikyumisaki is beautiful. We pass through the town of Muroran—its landed houses, barber shops and playgrounds. The road starts to slope upwards and we follow it all the way up to where the cliff meets the sea. The sky suddenly and dramatically opens up and you can see the calm blue of the Pacific Ocean. A sign says that Chikyumisaki is to our right. Lush green plants block our view to the sea again as we follow the sign.

Megumi keeps looking at the sky and at the trees.

"Are you looking for crows?" I ask her.

The smirk on her face says yes.

There are trees all around us, so Megumi's brown eyes are darting all over the place. I wonder what Muroran would look like when it's covered in snow. There's an older couple walking the same path in front of us, decked in hiking gear and backpacks. I start to wonder if all Japanese people have a set of hiking gear at home to go on trips like this. I've seen so many of them dressed identically throughout my journey. I feel slightly under-dressed in my black jacket.

All of us reach Chikyumisaki together. The small parking lot has ice cream shops and vending machines. Megumi buys a Hokkaido milk soft-serve cone for herself. I buy a can of coffee from the vending machine, finish drinking it and go to the public toilet which is on a landing leading up to the observatory. While I'm peeing, I hear a boy softly sobbing in one of the toilet stalls. I don't think much of it and wash my hands after I'm done. Just near the entrance is a sign that says—

"Beware of lost items!"

I let out a chuckle and read the phrase aloud. The sound of sobbing from inside the stall stops.

Megumi is waiting for me outside and is almost done with her soft-serve cone. I offer my services to finish off what's left of it. We walk together to the observatory. She holds my hand while we walk up there.

The lighthouse in Chikyumisaki is exactly like the one in my dreams. A short white tower with large glass windows and a white dome on top. It sits atop a small piece of land that juts out from the cape at a slight depression. There's a winding path from the observatory that leads to the lighthouse. In the background, the stark blue of the sky meets the deep blue of the ocean, forming a curved horizon. The old couple rings a bell at the observatory which is supposed to bring happiness to whomever rings it. Megumi rolls her eyes. I join her in the eye rolling. We both check our surroundings to see if anything is out of place. Everything looks normal. It's a breezy and pleasant day. There aren't any birds to be seen anywhere. No seagulls or crows or anything remotely resembling an animal capable of flight. We walk over to the gate leading to the lighthouse and see that it's locked.

"We'll probably need to wait until it's darker, when there aren't any people here."

I agree. We can't go hopping over gates to lighthouses when there are people who came here specifically to see the lighthouse. We buy some bottled water from the vending machines downstairs. Megumi and I sit down on a bench and wait for the sun to set.

"Why did you come to Japan again, Kiku?"

"I don't really know. I mean I like anime and Japanese shows and have been fascinated by the country for a long time. But it was more than that. I felt as if there was something calling me here. Like I had a purpose. Does it sound silly?"

"Maybe your purpose was to meet me", Megumi smirks, showing me her dimples again.

"Don't flatter yourself", I joke, even though I want it to be true.

She rolls her eyes at me this time.

"I don't know any more. It probably did sound weird when I first explained it to the people who cared to ask. But it doesn't seem that weird or silly now. I feel like this is where I'm supposed to be right now, like I belong in this moment. I'm not sure what's going to happen next, but whatever it is, it needs to happen. Maybe there's something inside that lighthouse, maybe there isn't. But I need to see."

Megumi puts her head on my shoulder and strokes my hand. "Keep talking", she nudges me.

"You know, almost all my life, as far as I can remember, I've been taking medication so I would stop "seeing things that aren't there". I hear voices in my head that aren't mine, or remember things that never happened. I was diagnosed with mild schizophrenia as a child and I don't remember the last time I've gone so long without my antipsychotic medication. My whole life I've felt nothing but numbness. Well, there's the anxiety too, but mostly numbness. And if there was anything before the numbness, then I've forgotten it. One of my biggest fears is that there will come a day when I forget who I am. Like this, right now, the both of us sitting on this bench, will be lost forever. I don't want to forget. Because if I do, then my life would be meaningless. All of this would have meant nothing. I would just be a husk, taking up space, things going in and out of me without sticking."

I pause to think about what I just said. Would I even remember this conversation? I can already feel it turning to mush inside my head, the order of the sentences jumbling up, the meaning be…

"Kiku", Megumi says suddenly, breaking my chain of thought, "we never forget anything. Everything that you've experienced, you carry it with you. Your body and your soul remember everything. You will never forget this conversation. This bench. This sky."

The sky is a lighter shade of blue now, fading into pink. The clouds are glowing with the coolness of the blue as well as the warmth of the pink. It's hard to say where the blue ends and the pink begins. All I can say is that the sky is vast and beautiful.

"It's beautiful, isn't it?" she asks me.

"Yes, it's the most beautiful sky I've ever seen."

"A long time ago, my foster father, Jiji, told me that the most beautiful skies in Japan can be found in Kagoshima. There are islands off its coast that haven't changed much in the past thousand years and won't change in the next thousand years either. There is one island in particular, lost to the world, which has the most beautiful sky. The sky there is different. It's bigger than all the other skies. The only light that reaches that island is from the stars above. Jiji said that you can see the stars even in the daytime when you're there. At night, you see the entire Milky Way. And if you're ready to accept it, you can see your place in the universe."

I try to imagine my place in the universe—a tiny, insignificant atom.

"I've always wanted to go there, Kiku."

Her eyes are fixed on the sky.

"You're afraid that you'll forget this moment, aren't you? Then let's make a promise so that you never forget. Will you promise to go with me to that island, Kiku?"

"The sky island in Kagoshima?"

"Yes, the sky island in Kagoshima."

"I promise", I promise her, "And do you?"

"I promise", she promises.

The sun sets. The blues become indigoes and the pinks become violets. A beam of light cuts through the perfect sky. The lighthouse begins its daily routine of guiding ships to safety.

When you're out at sea for so long,

The lighthouse is a beacon of hope.

It's other purpose though,

Is to keep you from bashing into the rocks, Jojo says.

Before we head to the lighthouse, I go to the toilet again. As soon as I open the door, I let out a scream. There's a small grey boy standing in front of the door.

"Beware of lost items!" the sign above him proclaims calmly.

"Sorry", the boy says in English.

Megumi rushes to the toilet to find me frozen in terror. She sees that the boy is as scared of me as I am of him.

"I'm sorry", he says again and cowers in the corner with his hands shielding his head. All of him is grey in colour save for the flaming blue orb on top. He's an Aoirei.

"Kiku, it's ok", Megumi reassures me as she holds my hand tight to calm me down.

Something about the boy crouching in the corner and apologising like that reminds me of someone else I used to know. Who was it? Someone in school?

The boy looks up and asks in English, "Can you also speak English?"

"Yes, both of us can", Megumi replies to him. "What's your name?"

The boy looks stunned, his mouth agape.

"You can hear me?"

I calm my breathing, "Yes, we can hear you. My name is Kiku. This is my friend, Megumi."

"I'm Jin!" the boy replies, looking positively thrilled. In an instant his excitement turns into worry as he asks us, "Have you seen my parents? I can't find them."

I look at Megumi not knowing what to say.

"What are their names, Jin-chan? Do you remember?" Megumi asks him.

For a brief moment his face lights up again, as if he's remembered something important. His blue soul glows brighter and then fades back to being pale blue.

"Otousan[16] and okasan[17]", he replies, dejected by his own answer.

"That's ok. Do you remember coming here with your otousan and okasan?"

"I came here with them. They said they were going to the toilet together. I followed the crow to the lighthouse. The crow said he would eat me."

Crows again.

"What do you want to do Jin-chan?" Megumi asks him.

"I want to find my parents", he sobs. The sobs soon turn into grey tears.

"And, where are they?"

"I don't know", he manages.

"Try to think, Jin-chan. Where do you think they are?"

"The lighthouse."

---

[16] *Otousan*—Father
[17] *Okasan*—Mother

"Do you want to go to the lighthouse?" Megumi asks.

"We can take you there", I add in, but Megumi signals me to not say anything.

"Do you want to go to the lighthouse, Jin-chan?"

"No. The crow will eat me."

"There are no crows outside, Jin-chan."

"No. The crow will eat me."

"No crows Jin-chan. I checked for them myself."

"No, I don't want to go!" he screams.

"What are you really afraid of, Jin?" Megumi asks forcefully.

Jin runs through the wall to the other side where the urinals are. Megumi shakes her head, slightly frustrated by the exchange.

"He's really scared", she explains.

"Can I try and talk to him?" I ask Megumi.

"Ok", she agrees, "but he must find his own answers. Do you understand?"

"Maybe. But let me try", I insist. Megumi reluctantly nods her head. I head to the urinals and see him crouched in the corner again. Where have I seen this before? I walk slowly up to him and crouch down beside him.

"Jin-chan", I say gently, "would you like to go home?"

"Yes", he sobs.

"Are you afraid of going home?"

"Yes", he sobs.

"Are you afraid of the crow?"

"Yes, he wants to eat me."

"Are you afraid of your father?" I ask, suddenly. I don't know why my own father pops into my head.

"Yes."

"Me too", I say, "My father and I don't talk much. He doesn't even know I'm here."

"My father told me not to go to the lighthouse", Jin replies.

I reach my hand out to pat his head but my hand goes straight through him. Jin sees the gesture and stretches his arms out to hug me. I stretch my arms out too. I feel him go inside. I shudder. In an instant, my world goes blue.

I'm playing with my favourite car on my father's desk. Father told me not to touch anything so I'm careful about where I drive my car. I drive my car around his lighter. I drive around his glass paper weight. It's so shiny! I drive to his pe…

His fountain pen is open. Where is the cap? Did I drop it on the floor while playing?

Am I thinking in Japanese?

I'm searching for the cap. I have the pen in my right hand and car in my left hand. Where is the cap? I can't find it. Should I use the pen to see if the ink is dry? I can write on a piece of paper to see. I climb up to his desk again and write on his notepad. The ink isn't coming out. I think I should shake it.

In my mind I see a tiny hand shaking the fountain pen violently. Is that my hand?

OH NO! I got, ink on my father's shirt. There's ink on the bed too. What should I do, what should I do?

I can feel myself panicking.

The door opens and father walks in.

"What did you do you stupid boy?" he's shouting. He's coming to hit me. He's coming to hit me!

I feel a sharp slap on my face and I fall onto the toilet floor.

"Why are you such a burden all the time? Do you know what you have done to my life? Do you know how much I regret getting your mother pregnant? If only I hadn't gone to that stupid lighthouse. Then I wouldn't have to deal with you! I wouldn't have so many burdens in my life!"

I start crying. Or is it Jin who's crying? I can't tell any more.

I don't want to be a burden, father. I don't want to be a burden. I won't be a burden.

I won't be a burden.

I won't be a burden.

I won't be a burden, I promise to myself.

"You're not a burden", I'm sobbing on the toilet floor.

"I won't be a burden", Jin is crying, also laying on the toilet floor, just like me.

Megumi walks over and sits next to Jin.

"I won't be a burden.

I won't be a burden.

I won't be a burden."

She puts her hand on his head. They touch. And then she says to him—

"You are as real as the rain that does not fall.

You live, yet you are not alive.

You seek the way because you are lost.

And in the darkness I am your guide."

The cold air becomes warm. Jin's grey tears turn into blue. Out they come, flowing from his eyes, steaming in the air. These are the tears of his soul. His blue flame glows bright, bathing the entire toilet in its blue light. The brilliant blue colour is warm and familiar. I feel it inside me, glowing too. The sweet smell of mint leaves fills my lungs. Megumi casts me a quick glance and then settles her eyes back on Jin.

Jin cries his heart out. After he’s done and the tears stop, Megumi asks him, "I am your Guide now, Jin-chan. Are you ready to go?"

"Yes", Jin replies.

The sky is black and full of stars. The lighthouse cuts through it with a broad swath of golden light. I help Jin over the gate leading to the lighthouse, then Megumi and then myself. Jin, Megumi and I walk down the zig-zag path, hand in hand. I feel his tiny hand in mine, cold and paper like. He looks up and smiles at me as I give it a little squeeze.

"The crow is gone", Jin says to me, smiling.

"The crow will never get you", I promise him.

We stop in front of the lighthouse door. I pick Jin up so that he can reach the door handle. He turns it and the door opens. We step inside together.

18. The Forgotten Forest

We step through the lighthouse door and into a thick forest. Amber light pours through the canopy of leaves. The trees are thick and tall, like they've been there for thousands of years. They probably have. The forest floor is covered in yellowing grass and maple leaves. I look up again and the trees are now dark and twisted maple trees, their branches mangled and intertwining. Red sunlight filters through their fiery red leaves. I feel like I'm in a dream, the forest floor getting brighter and darker as the wind weaves a circuitous path through the branches, singing a mournful song.

I'm alone. Did I come here with someone? I see both my hands outstretched as if I'm searching for hands to hold. How silly of me. I let out a chuckle. The forest chuckles with me. Silly Kiku, of course you came here alone. You've always been alone.

Something about the forest feels oddly familiar. I've been here before, haven't I?

Yes, you have, Jojo, the forest replies.

Silly forest.

I take out my phone to see where I am but the battery is flat. Ah well, I say to myself and start walking. The grass and the fallen leaves crush gently beneath my feet. I smell the woody, dizzying smell of a thousand maple leaves in the air. I stretch my arms out to feel the cool and rough bark of the unknown trees that switch between being unknown and being maple. I really need to learn more about trees, I say out loud. The forest sulks and doesn't reply.

I see a clearing up ahead where golden sunlight is pouring through.

"Kiku", someone is calling me from far away.

I step into the sunlight and feel it's warmth wash over my skin and my face and my hair and my lips. Its warmth washes over my heavy eyelids and rejuvenates them. When I open them again, the forest is green and orange, instead of yellow. Orange Gulmohar buds litter the forest floor. I pick one up and crush it between my fingers to smell its sweet nectar.

How was school today, the forest asks me.

School? I was in Muroran just now on a holiday. Why would I be in school? The forest is being silly again. One by one I pick up the Gulmohar buds and crush them between my fingers. One by one. One by one. I lose myself to the single-minded task of smelling each and every bud that has fallen on the forest floor.

"Kiku, come back", someone whispers from far away.

The forest grows darker. The sun must be about to set or must've set already. I look around and see a gate that is covered in vines which wasn't there before. Or has it always been there? There's nothing behind the gate, only more forest. I walk up to it and start climbing over the gate. An Aoirei suddenly runs straight through me.

"Fuck! You cheating ghost! You're not allowed to run through objects!" I shout as I jump over the gate.

The Aoirei turns around to face me. His eyes are hollow and he's smiling a manic grin. Black liquid starts oozing out of his eyes. Black feathers sprout from his body. His teeth are razor sharp, his tongue—black. The 'flaming' orb above his head is smoky and black, like a lump of coal, burning without a flame. Two large black wings spread out behind him, blinding me with their shimmering, liquid blackness. The thing recognises me.

"Welcome back, Jojo", he crows in his guttural, familiar voice.

"RUN, KIKU!" Megumi shouts. I turn around and run full sprint.

The creature behind me lets out a blood curdling scream. Electricity runs through my skin and every single hair on my body stands up. I dare not turn around to see what's coming behind me. I hear the whooping of large wings with the fluttering of a thousand smaller wings close behind.

"Don't stop for anything, Kiku!" Megumi shouts, "Don't stop for anything!"

I don't stop for anything.

"Run towards my voice, Kiku!" Megumi is shouting.

In my mind, I see her azure blue yukata with icy maple leaf patterns crisscrossing everywhere. I see her face half buried in a pillow, a single brown eye looking straight at me. I see us floating into a star-filled sky on a forgotten island. I remember our promise.

And then I see her, running towards me, in her blue cardigan and black jeans. Her short brown hair, flying behind her. The screaming behind me grows louder. I stretch every last muscle in my body and reach out to her. We collide violently and land in front of the lighthouse door. The screaming stops.

I'm gasping for breath and shivering. Megumi is clutching her chest and dry-heaving. We lay there on the ground for a while, panting, catching our breath. A yellow beam of light keeps blinding me. The ocean waves crash gently on the rocks somewhere. We're back in Muroran.

"Where was that?" I manage.

"The Forgotten Forest", she gasps. "I'm sorry Kiku, I shouldn't have taken you with me. I've never stepped into the forest with another living person before, except for Jiji. I guided Jin to the village. Natsu ba-chan[18]... well, this time Natsu-chan, would take care of him there."

"But I lost track of you! " she adds with a whimper, "I'm so sorry! I'm so so sorry!"

---

[18] *Ba-chan* or *Oba-chan*—Grandmother

I crawl over to Megumi and hug her, "Hey, hey, it's ok. We're back now. You brought me back. See?"

I point to the sky.

"Yokatta[19]", she sighs as we both take a moment to gaze at the star-filled sky above us.

"What was that thing that chased me?"

"He is the Master. And the crows are his minions. He would've torn you apart, Kiku, and eaten your soul."

"He knew me."

"It's possible. When you pass through The Forgotten Forest, you eventually reach The Village of Lost Souls, Tochuu. I've guided many Aoirei to its gates. Maybe you were a Guide too in your past life? Maybe that's why the Master knows you? He is hungry for souls and the lost Aoirei are low hanging fruits for him, ripe for the picking."

Welcome back, Jojo, he had greeted me.

"The Forgotten Forest is a dangerous place if you aren't prepared. It can show you things you aren't ready to see. Confuse you and seduce you. It was foolish of me to let you step through without explaining where we were headed. Some Aoirei find their way to the forest by themselves. Others need a guide, like Jin. You never know 'when' you will end up in. Tochuu and the forest exist outside of time. Or at least outside of our limited understanding of what 'time' means. Time is fluid in that space. The past, the present, the future and the eternal, collapse on top of each other."

"Wibbly-wobbly, timey-wimey", I say as I channel my inner Doctor Who[20].

Megumi stares at me with a serious face. And then we both burst into

---

[19] *Yokatta*—Thank goodness
[20] *Doctor Who*—British sci-fi TV show that involves a lot of time travel

laughter. We roll on the grass, clutching our stomachs. I laugh at the ridiculousness of it all. The Forgotten Forest, Tochuu, it all sounds so ridiculous. And yet, why does it sound plausible? Familiar even? I must be losing my mind. I *am* losing my mind. I'm losing my mind in the middle of nowhere, underneath a lighthouse that opened up to a forest. What could be more ridiculous than that?

The fact that I'm loving all of it.

19. Omkara

Omkara wipes the blood and sweat off his face. It's beautiful, his latest creation. He has stitched the entire family into a beautiful carpet of skin and flesh. Mother, father, son and daughter will be together forever, like all families are supposed to, woven into each other's lives and bodies. He uses their bones to stretch the canvas of skin and guts. Quite the artist he is. And quite famous too. The "Khooni Darjee[21]" they call him in the newspapers. Omkara hates the comical name but doesn't mind the attention.

"1997—The Year of The Khooni Darjee", reads out Omkara to the close-knit family of four. He adjusts his gold framed reading glasses with one gloved hand and straightens the newspaper with another.

In a shocking series of murders all over India that has left the police baffled, the serial killer known as The Khooni Darjee has cut through the very fabric of Indian consciousness. Committing acts of grisly murders on innocent families, he leaves no trace behind, police say.

Having killed 31 families so far, in 15 cities…

"32 families in 16 cities", Omkara interjects.

…the only pattern all the murders have are that they're being committed on middle-class nuclear families and that the murderer dismembers the bodies and arranges them in horrifying patterns that are too shocking to be printed. All the murders have been committed inside the family's homes, with no survivors or witnesses.

The CID has been tasked with the challenge of uniting the cross-state police investigations to bring this vile criminal to justice.

---

[21] *Khooni Darjee*—Killer tailor

The article goes on but the family isn't paying any attention to him. They're just happy to be together again.

"Well, my work here is done."

Omkara takes off his full body 'murdering' raincoat, gloves and the plastic bags tied to his feet and neatly folds them into a large 'Fakeeza' plastic bag. Fakeeza store is all the rage in the city of Indore and a convenient place to shop for clothes to murder in. He takes out his other raincoat, the one meant for cleaning, and places it on the floor for later use. Next, he strips off his normal clothes and walks to the bathroom to bathe himself.

He spends the next two hours scrubbing—himself, then the bathroom and then every nook and cranny of the house where he may have left a stray hair or dead skin or God forbid, a fingerprint. He takes special care of the cupboard safe from which he has helped himself to all the money and jewellery inside. He checks his watch—16:44. The milkman will be here around 18:00, so he needs to wrap up soon. His bus to Nagpur leaves at 21:45. Omkara collects all the trash, compresses it neatly and stuffs it into his large backpack that he bought for today's excursion. Everything else, his knives, scissors, sewing kit, other murder paraphernalia and his spoils from the family cupboard, he keeps in his smaller bag. He leaves using the front gate, wiping everything he touches with the deft motions of his trained surgeon hands.

On the way to the bus station, he takes a quick detour to an open garbage dump, one of many in Indore, and burns the large backpack along with everything inside it. Nobody casts him a second glance.

His bus to Nagpur arrives forty five minutes late, which is surprisingly early by Indori standards. Vomit streaks mark the sides of the bus in parallel lines. It drops off its previous batch of greasy human cargo to make room for Omkara and the next batch of human cargo to be greased. Omkara finds a relatively clean seat next to a shy and timid looking boy. The bus leaves two hours later than the original time of 21:45—which is exactly on time in Indore.

The young boy, probably no older than seven, is listening to songs on a battered old Walkman with blue headphones that cover his ears. Omkara snaps his fingers in front of the boy's face which jolts the headphones off him.

"Hi there, little boy. I'm Vishnu. What's your name?" Omkara enquires, obviously lying about his name.

"I'm Ganesh. Pleased to meet you, sir", the boy replies politely.

"Wow, such a fantastic name you have, master Ganesh! Lord Ganesh! The God of intellect and wisdom. The God of new beginnings! Very good, master Ganesh, very good indeed!"

The boy manages a shy smile.

"Where are your parents, Ganesh? Are you travelling alone?"

"I'm going to meet them in Nagpur. They adopted me."

"Oh, my word! A fellow orphan! Such fateful coincidence this is, that we might be seated together. However, I was never as fortunate as you, master Ganesh, to be adopted by a loving family. One must count their blessings. Isn't that so?"

The boy nods politely.

"And even though this may seem like a fateful coincidence, there are no such things as coincidences, are there?"

The boy shakes his head.

"You're a very bright young boy, I see. And brave too, travelling all by yourself. Who knows what kinds of horrible people you might meet along the way? How lucky for you then that you should find a gentleman, such as myself, as your co-passenger."

The boy seems to have lost interest in the conversation. It's apparent from his blank face that he just wants to get back to listening to his music. Omkara wonders if he should follow the boy back to his new home in Nagpur and help him "settle in". Nagpur is only a stopover to convert some jewellery into cash, but he could stay a few extra days to get to know the locals. He looks at the boy who has his blue headphones on again, lost in his own world. He can hear the faint traces of an English song leaking through the perforated old sponge. It's a familiar tune. Right! It's that cheesy love song from Titanic that keeps playing on the radio all the time, Omkara exclaims to himself. He looks at the boy again and feels a sense of kinship towards him. On his own, this brave young boy is venturing into the unknown, off to a foreign city. He would have to carve his own path, cut himself a piece of the love that his biological parents denied him. Omkara wonders if the boy has gone through the horrors that he himself had gone through. Gone through and overcame, Omkara shouts in his own head. The boy can overcome such adversities too, he's sure. Omkara can show the boy the way. What if he can influence the boy and have a partner in crime that he can train from a young age? There are no such things as coincidences, after all. Maybe the boy has been placed here for a reason. Maybe he can take the boy with him on a wonderf…

Buffalo enters the road.

The driver sees the buffalo too late and drives straight into it.

The front of the bus collapses in on itself like an accordion. The driver and buffalo are the first ones to die. The buffalo is flung inside the bus and kills the first row of passengers instantly. Chunks of buffalo and metal fly through the air and impale anyone unfortunate enough to be in their trajectory. The Khooni Darjee receives a buffalo horn in his throat. The bus, its greasy old passengers and greasy new passenger dance through the night sky. Omkara's world is going dark. His throat feels numb. He sees the boy floating in the air, blue headphones and all, his mouth wide open. Their eyes meet. Omkara wonders what it would be like to fly into the boy's mouth right about now. He lets out a gurgled chuckle at his absurd last thoughts on earth. There's no white light. His life doesn't flash before his eyes. There's only an ever-growing darkness. And just before the darkness takes him, everything turns blue.

The cold Malwa air wakes him up. His head feels like a road-roller has run over it. His body moves of its own accord. Hey, what are you doing right hand? Why are you moving on your own? His left hand feels for the buffalo horn.

It's not there.

Something feels odd. He looks at his hands. They're covered in cuts and scrapes. There's a bone jutting out of the right one. More importantly though, they're tiny! Like a child's hand! Omkara and Ganesh panic.

Why am I so tiny now Who is this WHAT DID YOU DO TO ME Who am I Let me out Who are we

Neither knows which one is speaking. Each voice tries to drown out the other. Ganesh's tiny body starts shaking from the trauma of accommodating two souls when there's room for only one. His (Their) eyes roll over and he (they) fall(s) into a deep coma.

20. Hakodate

I love big burgers and I cannot lie. Big fat juicy ones.

And Lucky Pierrot has arguably the best burgers in all of Hokkaido and maybe the whole world. I'm gobbling burger after burger at the Bay Area outlet of Lucky Pierrot in Hakodate. Each burger seems to be made with love and tenderness, packed with umami. Megumi is laughing her ass off as she watches me wolf them down between sips of coke and gasps of pure satisfaction.

After guiding young Jin to The Village of Lost Souls, Tochuu, we decided to spend the day in the nearby city of Hakodate. The moment I stepped off the train and saw the cute trams that run through the heart of this small port city, I fell in love. Hakodate has a charming mixture of Japanese and European architecture. It has trams, ports, bridges, sloping streets with shrines on top, ropeways and beautiful parks. And fantastic burgers.

"Are you done yet?" Megumi laughs.

I stare at her vacantly.

"Food coma, arh?" she tries to imitate my Singlish.

"I'm in heaven", I tell her, smiling.

"This isn't heaven, Kiku. Wait till we go up the ropeway at night", she winks.

I close my eyes and imagine what it must be like up there.

"Don't fall asleep now."

"Let me go! I've had the perfect meal."

"Meals you mean!"

"Yes, perfect meals."

I open one eye to see her smirking at me. I love her smirk, one side of her lip slightly curling up.

"So, what do we do next?" she asks me.

"Let's go and buy a suit."

"What?"

"You said I'd look sexy in a suit. So, let's go and buy one."

"I said that?"

"Yes, you did! In Muroran!"

She laughs and admits that she doesn't remember saying that to me but that I'd certainly look great in a black suit.

We head to Goryokaku and look for stores to buy a suit from. After some searching, we find one that has a sale going on. I buy a black suit for myself, black jacket, black tie and black pants. I buy a white shirt to complete the ensemble.

"I look like a waiter", I tell Megumi.

"You look like a sexy waiter. Mind keeping the suit on for me?"

"Sure", I wink.

We spend the rest of the day, me in my new suit, in and out of trams, holding hands, laughing.

"I can't wait to get back to our hotel room", she winks at me.

I feel a tightness in my chest. My right hand clenches and unclenches.

"Listen, Megumi. Do you mind if we take it a little slow? I feel anxious every time I think about sex. I get uncomfortable and nervous thinking about it."

"Did something happen?"

"I don't know. I mean, when I was in college, I had a girlfriend. I was mostly high on medication back then so the sex came and went and it neither excited me nor bothered me. With you though, I feel more…present? Is that the word you use sometimes? Well, I feel like I'm more here than I usually am. Does it make sense?"

"Yes, it makes sense. We'll take it at your pace", she says as she squeezes my hand. "What else did you see in the forest, Kiku?" she asks.

"I don't remember clearly, but I saw a gate that was covered in vines. It looked familiar. Was that something out of my memory?"

"Yes, it probably was. The forest is meant to prepare you for your journey into the Well of Memories. It will show you the memories that you've forgotten or hidden away inside your mind. Everyone has a different experience in the forest. Sometimes you see nothing. Sometimes you're confronted with the things you least want to see."

"What's the Well of Memories?"

"It's a gigantic well in the middle of Tochuu. There are steps along the side of it that lead to the bottom, if there is a bottom. The Aoirei make their final journey in the well. No one knows what's inside it, except maybe Jiji. But he's very cryptic about it and speaks in riddles. The forest is meant to prepare you for it, he often says."

"You've been through the forest many times, haven't you? What do you see?"

"It depends. When I'm alone, I sometimes see the men I've slept with. I don't see their faces, but I see their bodies having sex with my body. The sight of it makes me feel ashamed. Sometimes the forest is flooded with heavy rain. I see worms and scorpions and maggots emerging from the forest floor. When I see them, I feel cold and hungry. Like I did while I waited for my mother. When I'm guiding an Aoirei through the forest, I usually don't see anything. Sometimes the Aoirei see things from their past life and want to stop. I help them get past those things and guide them all the way to the village. For some, it takes days. In the case of Jin, it took less than an hour. His life was short and his traumas were on the surface. You helped him see one of them in Muroran."

I frown thinking about it.

"I've never seen anything like that, Kiku. When you hugged him, he went inside you. It was as if you both became one. I could hear his voice coming through your mouth. I must admit, it was creepy. But I could tell that he was facing something he had run away from. Somehow, going inside you unlocked that memory for him."

I won't be a burden, Jojo repeats.

"I couldn't tell who was who. It was as if my brain kept switching between two people. I heard my voice which felt like it was mine and also not mine."

A bolt runs through me.

"You know, I've often felt like I have memories that don't belong to me. Voices that don't belong there. Could it be that I'm possessed by an Aoirei?"

Megumi laughs, "No Kiku, you're not possessed. I feel two souls inside you, but they live in harmony. Possession would imply that something went inside you without your consent. It's almost like a rape. It's not entirely unheard of—people being possessed by Aoirei. But there's always a struggle for control. In your case though, the struggle you feel is within your own soul and not caused by the other."

"Within my own soul, huh?"

"Yes", she blinks wisely.

It makes sense. Somewhat.

"What's the village like?" I ask.

"You'll see. I have a feeling that our journey will lead us there. I wonder 'when' we will end up in when we go. Time works differently there. Sometimes you end up in the past. Like when I guided Jin there, I saw a young Natsu-chan, maybe eleven years old. She's the Guardian of the village and my foster-mother. When she raised me, she was much older. It's a weird feeling to see your foster-mother suddenly younger than you are.

I've never seen a young Jiji though. I think he's always been old. He told me that you always end up exactly 'when' you're supposed to end up in Tochuu. I guess Jin was supposed to end up in the past of the village, if there is such a thing as the past for that place. Wibbly-wobbly timey-wimey."

We both laugh. I kiss her on the forehead.

That night we take the ropeway to the top of Hakodate-yama. The city spreads out, gleaming and glittering underneath us. Megumi laughs that Hakodate looks like a pair of panties from up here. It's shaped like a Y with water on both sides of the stem. I enjoy the view but don't enjoy the crowd. We make an early exit back to our hotel room.

As we lie in bed, I ask her, "Is it weird for you to be in bed with someone and not having sex?"

"Umm…a little bit. Usually the guys can't keep their hands off me."

"I can imagine. I'm sorry."

"You don't have to be Kiku. I like this."

"I like this too", I admit.

We spend the night talking in bed between bouts of kissing and cuddling. The sky turns from black to purple. As the sun starts to rise, we fall asleep holding each other.

21. Natsu

Natsu bolted through the trees. Her feet were covered in blisters but it was almost sundown. She had spent too long in the Forgotten Forest, chasing rabbits for dinner. And now she might not make it back in time. There was no point in crying, she realized. She had to keep running till she reached the village, blisters or not. Her small lungs hurt from inhaling the cold autumn air in rushes and gasps. But in her mind, she was already planning which incense sticks to light first. She was running towards the sunset so the northern gates would be the closest. After lighting those incense sticks she would make a sprint towards the southern gates, cutting through the village. Only two gates to light. That's all she needed to do at sundown every day. And she had managed to make a mess of it today.

Not yet.

She slapped herself hard in the face. The pain woke her up from the lethargy of feeling sorry for herself. She lengthened her strides as she dashed through the forest.

As the trees gave way to shrubs, she could see the northern torii gates to her left. Each pole had a thick rice rope wrapped around it, the two mighty ropes encircling the village all the way around to the southern gates. The sun was almost at the horizon now. She extended her fingers in front of her eyes, trying to steady them to check how many fingers were left to sundown. One. Two if she was lucky.

She made a sharp turn to the left, using her left hand to steady herself as she almost fell to the ground. There were thickets of trees all along the perimeter of the village, the shimenawa[22] ropes appearing and disappearing

---

[22] *Shimenawa*—"Enclosing ropes" are lengths of laid rice straw or hemp rope used for ritual purification in the Shinto religion. They can vary in diameter from a few centimetres to several metres, and are often seen festooned with shide. A space bound by shimenawa often indicates a sacred or pure space, such as that of a

through the trunks, adorned with white shide[23] strips shaped like hollow squares instead of the usual lightning shapes. She could hear the birds chattering overhead as they made their way back to their nests. She heard the starlings, sparrows and thrushes tittering. She tried to listen harder but her own ragged breath and throbbing face made it difficult to concentrate. She hadn't been trained to listen to the birds while running full sprint. Clearly an oversight. She almost ran into the tall red torii gates of the north as she opened the wooden box at its foot to take out the incense sticks and the flint to light them with. The incense sticks were small but they could burn all night. She had made them herself, with her own blood. She was careful not to let her sweat drip on them as she placed one of them at the base of the left pillar and lit it. When she turned around to reach the other pillar, she heard a loud caw.

Natsu froze in her tracks. To her right was a crow. And it was sitting in the middle of the path Natsu had just run down, looking at her inquisitively. Natsu stared at the crow. The crow stared back.

"Muda[24]", the crow cawed.

A bolt of lightning ran through her body as Natsu sprang back to life and rushed to the other pillar. She glanced to her right again as she placed the incense stick in the ground. The crow wasn't there. She could still see the light of the setting sun so it hadn't entered the village. It couldn't have. She still had time. She lit the second stick and began running again, through the forested path leading into the village.

She could see faint glows of blue ahead of her. The floating orbs of flame almost looked like blue fireflies from this distance. The sun had probably set by now, but the sky was still orange. It was a small village with only forty four houses in it. Out of the forty four, there was only one house that had any furnishings. That's where old Jiji and Natsu lived. She wondered where old Jiji was right now as she ran past her home. He had gone to bring supplies from the mortal world and she was to take care of

---

Shinto shrine.
[23] *Shide*—A zigzag-shaped paper streamer, often seen attached to shimenawa
[24]*Muda*—Useless, futile

the Aoirei by herself. There were no other living beings in the village of Tochuu except for Jiji and herself. At that time at least. And that made it all the more important for her to fulfil her duty as Guardian to the lost and wandering Aoirei who seemed to find their way into Tochuu. As she ran past them, their pale puzzled faces illuminated by their blue souls, she wondered if she would become an Aoirei too one day. What a sad and cold thought it was. She could see the Well of Memories now in the centre of the village, its spiralling steps leading down into an infinite darkness. The well was so enormous that a hundred men could stand around its circumference, hand in hand, and still not complete the circle. As she ran past it she peeked inside to check for any blue flickers. There were none. Maybe no one had made the walk today.

The sky was getting dark now. The last streaks of orange had become pink and were soon going to fade to cobalt.

"Natsu-kun!" someone called out to her. But she had no time to waste and kept running south. She heard the starlings, sparrows and thrushes tittering away once again. But this time there was also the distinct cawing of a crow. Only one, she counted.

She could see the southern torii gate ahead of her now. Between her and the gate was young Jin, the newest addition to Tochuu, his soul glowing bright blue. He was smelling the rose bushes again, like he had done every day ever since he had arrived. They reminded him of his mother, he had said.

"Jin-chan! Run away! Jin-chan!"

As Jin turned to face Natsu, the last lights in the sky faded away. There was a low rumbling caw. A large black figure landed on top of Jin and pinned him to the ground with large talons. The Karasu was covered in black feathers, its body an unholy amalgamation of man and crow. Where there should have been feet, there were claws. Where there should have been a face there was a razor sharp beak and dark liquid eyes. It had human like arms but they were too black and covered in feathers to belong to anything human. And the large wings on its back were dark, shimmering and mesmerizing. Natsu's eyes were transfixed on its wings as the Karasu tore Jin's head off like a tasty piece of bread and swallowed it whole. It ate the rest of his body, piece by piece, until only his soul remained, the blue flaming orb that had been glowing ever so fiercely as his metaphysical body disappeared into the belly of the ravenous beast. The Karasu pecked at it with obvious relish. It picked it up between its beaks and looked at Natsu with cold liquid eyes. And with one solid gulp, Jin was gone. Only darkness remained.

"I told him I would eat him", the Karasu said flatly.

Natsu realized her face had been streaming with tears. The temperature was dropping in the forest and the chill cut her deep. She looked at the Karasu staring at her quizzically. More crows would gather soon. She knew what she needed to do. Old Jiji had taught her. She took out the small skinning knife she had been carrying on her side all day. She extended her left palm in front of her so that the Karasu could see exactly what she was about to do. With one swift swipe she slashed deep into her palm. Hot blood fell on the ground. Hot blood dripped down Natsu's left hand, staining her blouse red. Hot blood steamed in the cold autumn air.

"Disgusting", crowed the Karasu.

Natsu took a step forward.

The Karasu calmly turned around and flapped its giant ebony wings several times. The dazzling blacks shimmered and disappeared in front of Natsu's eyes as she saw a small crow fly away, cawing incessantly. All that was left in front of her was a puddle of black feathers. Sullen with tears, she stepped over them and made her way to the southern gate to light the remaining incense sticks.

22. The Man in Black

Ever since his last flight into the forest, Ganesh has stopped flying when he sleeps. His body won't let him go. Instead, he dreams every night—heavy and colourful dreams. The kind of dreams that leave your ears blocked and your head buzzing when you eventually wake up from them. In these dreams he sees thieves and robbers, mutilated bodies being sown into complex sculptures, knives glinting in the moonlight, blue flaming orbs and overturned buses.

There's a knock on his bedroom door.

"Ganesh, there's someone here to see you", his father says through the door.

Ganesh gets dressed and goes downstairs to the living room. His mother is serving tea and biscuits to a man dressed in a black suit. It's unusual to see anyone dressed in a suit. Especially in India. Especially in Nagpur.

"Two for the price of one", the man muses as he sees Ganesh walk in. He's in his fifties, probably, and doesn't look Indian. Ganesh can't quite seem to place his ethnicity. He has a long face and sunken eyes. He has dark black hair that sits messily atop his head, covering most of his forehead. There's something about the man's eyes that's deeply unsettling. His corneas are jet black.

"Hi, do I know you?" Ganesh asks the man in black.

"No, Mr. Desai, but I know you very well. Or should I say, I know your *work* very well."

"You can call me Ganesh. Mr. Desai would be my father."

"Your step-father you mean."

The man's face remains expressionless as he says this.

"Yes, I was adopted. Are you from the orphanage?"

"No, Mr. Desai. Ganesh. I'm from the CID[25]."

The man takes out a badge and flashes it to Ganesh. Ganesh feels a lump in his throat. He does the best poker face he can muster up. He feels one side of his face twitching.

"We've been following your work quite closely, Ganesh. The job you did in the Gupta farmhouse was quite extraordinary", the man in black says as he sips his tea.

Ganesh starts checking off his mental checklist.

Was I followed? No.

Were there any cameras in the farmhouse? No.

When I fed the dogs, were there any cars following me? No.

He had been very careful. What exactly did this man know about the farmhouse?

"I see that you're confused Ganesh. Maybe you'd like to talk more in my car. I'm sure you don't want us to create a ruckus in front of your family. I have a team waiting outside the house, should you choose to be uncooperative. I myself am trained to handle such situations on my own. I promise not to use any deadly force on you unless I see you as a danger to my life. Or to that of your beloved family. You will cooperate of your own will, won't you Ganesh?"

"But I haven't done anything", Ganesh stammers.

"Oh Ganesh", the man in black sighs as he finishes his tea and places the cup neatly back in its saucer. He uses a handkerchief to wipe off the black marks his lips have left on the rim of the tea cup. He then takes a photograph and places it on the coffee table between him and Ganesh. Ganesh recognizes the woman in the photo. It's his third victim, Mrs. Malhotra, the lady who used to beat stray cats to death. Cold sweat appears

---

[25] *CID*—Criminal Investigation Department

on his nose and he wipes it off.

"The car is waiting outside. We can talk more on the way. It's very hot inside your living room, isn't it?"

"Where are you taking me?"

"That depends entirely on how cooperative you are, Ganesh. I could take you to a place where you never see the sun again, or I could take you for a short ride and drop you back home. It all depends on you."

"What should I tell my parents?"

"Tell them whatever you want. Or don't tell them anything at all. For now, just come with me. There's no need to take anything with you."

Ganesh gets up from his chair. He wonders if he can release his spirit in this very instant and let his body handle the consequences. He closes his eyes tight and tries to summon his spirit to fly. FLY, FLY, he's shouting in his mind.

"That won't work", the man in black whispers in his ear.

Outside, a black Mercedes is waiting for them. Inside are seated two other men wearing black. They look like the FBI agents that you see in movies. Dressed in black, black sunglasses on, not a single expression on their faces. Ganesh gets in the car and the man in black sits next to him in the back seat. The locks click in place and the car drives away. Ganesh looks back at his house. It's the last time he ever sees it again.

23. Lime Ice Cream

I'm surprised to see customers coming into La Porte. The last time I was here it was completely empty and tonight we have all four bar seats occupied. There's an old couple, a young girl and a salaryman. They all know Megumi and appear to be regulars. I've decided to help her in the kitchen by washing the dishes and utensils. I'm utterly useless when it comes to cooking. Washing dirty dishes is more up my alley and something that I find oddly therapeutic.

All the customers keep casting me side-eyed glances while they talk to Megumi.

"Who's that young man in your kitchen, Megumi-chan? Did you disappear to get married last week?" the old man chuckles. His wife elbows him and tries to stifle her own laughter.

"Well it's about time Megumi-san found a hardworking man. It must be lonely running this place by yourself. Isn't that so Megumi-san?" the salaryman joins in.

"Where's he from?" the young girl asks.

"I kidnapped him from Singapore", Megumi laughs.

I chuckle along. Megumi casts me a cheeky glance and asks, "What are you laughing about, Kiku?"

"I came of my own free will", I say.

The old man looks at me in amazement, "Wow! Can you speak Japanese, young man?"

"No", I reply in Japanese.

That's weird. I play back the conversation in my head and realize that they had been speaking in Japanese the entire time. When the hell did I learn Japanese?

Megumi's expression matches the old man's now.

"Kiku, I didn't know you spoke Japanese."

"Neither did I", I confess in Japanese. Is it because of Jin, I wonder.

"Come and join us", the old man says. I happily oblige.

The conversations flow late into the night. The patrons want to know everything about me and how is it that I can speak Japanese so fluently and what's Singapore like and wow, you've watched so many Japanese movies and so on and so forth. At some point I start talking about my travels (I leave out the supernatural elements). They seem to be more interested in the nature of my relationship with Megumi. I tell them that I don't fully understand what this is and that I enjoy spending time with her. The topic then shifts to love and relationships. By the time everyone starts to leave, it's almost 1am in the morning.

As I'm cleaning up the counter, the front door opens and an old man, dressed in a trench-coat and hat walks in. He strides straight to the counter and sits on the fourth seat. He avoids looking at me. Megumi steps out of the kitchen to see who it is.

"Megumi-chan", the old man says.

"Jiji! Would you like something to eat?" Megumi exclaims.

The old man shakes his head and slips a folded note across the counter. Then, without even a second glance he walks out of La Porte.

Megumi looks on, disappointed. She opens the note and reads what's inside.

"Was that your foster-father?" I ask.

"Yes, that was Jiji", she replies, still sour from his abrupt departure.

I hesitate to ask what's in the note but ask her anyway.

"It's a list of names and addresses. You see, I'm actually a hitman", she says to me with a straight face. She then starts laughing at her own joke.

"No lah, it's a list of places that have Aoirei that may need my help."

"I see. Are the places all in Hokkaido?"

"Yes, they are."

"What about the Aoirei in other parts of Japan? And other countries? Do you guide them too?"

"Jiji has a network of Guides. There aren't many of us from what I hear, but we're spread all over the world."

"Have you met any of the other Guides?"

"No, I haven't. Jiji doesn't talk much about the others and neither does Natsu. I don't know what the criteria is for one to be chosen as a Guide either. Being able to see the Aoirei is definitely one of them."

"Yeah, I can imagine it being an essential criteria", I chuckle.

We close shop around 2am in the morning. Megumi and I go to the nearby convenience store to buy some food. I buy melon bread to eat for breakfast. Megumi picks something out of the freezer.

We head back to her apartment. As soon as we're through the door, we start making out. I get nervous by its abruptness. Megumi senses the tension in me and slows down the pace of her kissing. We stand near her bed, caressing, kissing slowly. My mind wanders to the patrons of her diner. It then wanders to the old man, Jiji. He avoided looking at me. Why did it feel like I had seen him before? Megumi playfully bites my lips and brings me back. The mint leaf smell in her hair makes me feel giddy. I grab her by the waist. I feel my hand brushing over her face, tracing the shape of her ears, her jaw, her neck. She sighs as I trace my fingers under her neck and move my thumb against her chin. I feel my penis getting larger as she gently pulls on it with her thumb and forefinger, coaxing it through my jeans.

Clothes come off. Plastic bag gets thrown on her bedside table. We throw ourselves onto the bed which groans loudly.

Her breasts are round and soft, topped by soft nipples that harden at my touch. I pull on one gently and she lets out a soft moan. My lips start tracing a downward path, moving from her chin, to her warm neck, then to her collarbone. I stop there to bite them playfully, both collarbones in turn. It makes her laugh and it makes my movements bolder. Both my hands move with intent and purpose, one rubbing the wet lips of her vagina, slipping in and out, teasing her, while the other fondles her breast, rubbing her nipple with the thumb. Her own hands join in. I flick her other nipple with my tongue, gently sucking and nibbling, encouraged by how hard it is. She moans and arches her back. Her hips gyrate in tune with the motion of my fingers. All this time, my erection rubs against the inside of her thigh, dribbling everywhere. I reach for the drawer to take out a condom. While I put it on, I see Megumi looking at me, feverish lust in her eyes, like she wants to devour me whole. I'm suddenly aware of how heightened my senses are. I feel the cold air of the air-conditioner rush inside me as I breathe deeply. It makes the thin sheen of sweat on my skin tingle. I can smell her body, her aroma, the mint leaves in her hair. I kneel in front of her and pull her thighs forcefully to bring her body closer to mine. She lets out a yelp and then a laugh. She grabs hold of my penis and guides me inside her. The feeling of warmth envelops me. I start slowly, with gentle strokes. I look down at her heaving breasts but Megumi pulls my hair to make me look at her face instead. Her mouth is open and her breath is in sync with my own. Hot breath mixes together in the space between us. I let my arms relax and close in to kiss her mouth. We kiss and gasp, kiss and gasp as I start increasing my pace. Our bodies collide with each other, again and again and again. The gasps turn into moans and the moans turn into screams of pleasure. The bed squeaks and shakes and screams in tune with us. I feel a warmth rise to the surface. I need to slow down or I'll come soon.

My eyes move to the plastic bag on the table, inside are two packets of lime flavoured ice cream.

Just like the ones I used to bring for Johnny.

And then suddenly, the screams turn into sobs. I see a naked man sobbing in the corner.

"You looked inside! You looked inside me!" he's sobbing.

I start screaming and sobbing myself.

I DIDN'T MEAN TO LOOK!

I DIDN'T MEAN TO LOOK!

I DIDN'T MEAN TO LOOK!

I DIDN'T MEAN TO LOOK!

I DIDN'T MEAN TO LOOK!

And just like that, my world goes black.

24. Johnny

Johnny's favourite flavour of ice cream is lime. Lime! It's ridiculous. Who the hell likes lime ice cream? He says he can't eat them anymore but I still bring an extra stick for him anyway and then eat this abomination of an ice cream in front of him to tease him. I'm just messing around though.

We love exploring the old mansion he lives in together. It has many rooms in it and each one has a story behind it that Johnny likes to tell me at great lengths. The living room for instance is where his family was once held hostage by a couple of bumbling robbers one of whom, caught up in the excitement of the robbery, tripped over the carpet, broke his nose and bled all the way to the kitchen. The mango tree in the corner of the courtyard was where Johnny liked to secretly smoke so that his wife wouldn't find out. He loves his son's room. His son and he would spend hours playing with Lego there. I told Johnny that I love when my father brings home Lego from his overseas trips and that I have a formidable collection of my own. I asked if he wanted me to bring some of my Lego here, but he refused, saying that it would remind him too much of his son.

Behind the house, is a small thicket of trees where his son and wife are buried.

Michael & Marlynn D'Souza

Beloved Son & Mother

The Sun Shines Slightly Dimmer

Without Them Here

And next to their tombstone is another slightly smaller one—

Jonathan D'Souza

Beloved Father

May He Reunite With

His Family In Heaven

Clearly that didn't happen and Johnny ended up stuck in this shithole between heaven and hell with a blue flaming orb on top of his head. Johnny says that the blue orb is his soul. I've only ever touched it once and my hand felt strangely numb and uncomfortable as I did so. It neither had any heat nor any coldness to it. And just like the rest of Johnny, my hand passed straight through it.

Sometimes I wonder if Johnny is just a figment of my imagination. You know, to make me feel less like a loser without any friends. I've never had any real friends before. I used to know a boy called Ganesh but Raju told me that he ended up in a coma after a bus accident. I haven't told my father about Johnny or my visits to the old mansion. It's not like we talk much anyway and this would just be a good excuse for him to send me packing to a boarding school. Well, figment of imagination or not, he certainly feels real to me. He's a bit of a loner himself so he gets what I'm going through. I talk to him about school and my "friends" in the after-school music class I attend every Friday. He asked me why I chose to learn such an obscure instrument like the tabla[26] when there were hundreds of other things that girls would like better. I told him I chose it because I loved the smell of stinky socks in the tabla class! I was joking, of course.

On cloudy days we explore the neighbourhood together. I love exploring and drag Johnny along, even though he's a bit reluctant to stray too far away from his mansion. I, on the other hand, can't wait to escape from home and do so every chance I get. I asked my father to buy me a bicycle light on one of his overseas trips but he couldn't find one so I

---

[26] *Tabla*—A musical instrument of India consisting of a pair of drums whose pitches can be varied

usually just tape a torch light onto the handle of my bicycle and go night cycling. That's how I first found Johnny, on one of my night cycling expeditions, his blue orb dimly illuminating the courtyard of an abandoned mansion.

When I first entered the mansion to go and talk to him, he couldn't believe the fact that I could see him. He must've asked me a hundred times, "Can you really see me?" before we started a real conversation.

"Are you a ghost?" I asked him.

"I think so", he replied.

"You live here by yourself?"

"Yes, I do", he replied sadly.

"It's a huge mansion, you have here. Do you feel lonely?"

"Yes, all the time. Everyone I loved, left me behind."

I felt something squeezing at my heart when he said that. After that, somehow, the conversations flowed effortlessly. I promised to go and visit him from time to time, and I did. I would often go and meet him right after school. Our friendship grew as the days passed by.

Today we're exploring the other old buildings in the neighbourhood, a few lanes down. There are other people here, so I make it a point to not talk to Johnny while others are watching. Not that it matters if someone sees a ten year old boy "talking to himself", but there might be people from my school who live here.

"I knew some of the people who lived here before I passed. To be honest, I don't remember much about my death or when I ended up like this. I just know that everything is different now and everyone I knew or loved is long gone", laments Johnny. He walks soundlessly.

We walk past a tall and twisting Gulmohar tree, the wind rustling through its branches and littering the streets with flowers. I pick up an orange bud that fell near my feet and crush it between my fingers to smell its sweet nectar.

"How was school today?"

I shrug.

"Same as always?"

I nod.

"Did you speak to the cute girl sitting in front of you?"

"Sushmita? No", I blush and quickly look around to see if anyone saw me talk out loud.

"Don't worry, no one is around."

I look at Johnny. He's gently nodding his head from side to side and quietly smiling to himself. Just as I like to tease him with the lime ice creams, he likes to tease me about the girls in my class.

"I fell asleep in geography class again. Ms. Anita threw a chalk at me and called me a pumpkin", I chuckle in a low voice.

Johnny is looking at the sky which is covered in dark clouds.

"It might rain this afternoon, Johnny", I say.

"I'll race you back to the mansion!" he suddenly announces and starts his half floating sprint.

I laugh and start running after him at full speed. He's fast, but not faster than me. After all, I'm one of the fastest runners in my class, only second to Siddharth, who's much taller than I am. I overtake Johnny easily. I turn the corner to the mansion and slip on some loose gravel. It's not a bad fall, only a few scrapes. I pick myself up and keep running towards the gate that's covered in vines.

I climb over the gate while Johnny runs straight through me, laughing.

"Fuck! You cheating ghost! You're not allowed to run through objects!"

"Don't swear!" he laughs.

I'm panting and laughing myself. I catch up to him at the porch. He grins at me smugly, not a single drop of sweat on him. He looks like a black and white movie star who stepped straight through the silver screen and into reality, devoid of all colour save for his pale blue "soul". His face, his hair, his hands, his shirt, khaki pants and tweed jacket are all different shades of grey and all from a different era. He sees me staring and his smug grin dissolves into a concerned look.

"Hey, are you ok? You had a pretty bad fall."

"I'm fine."

"You cut your lip! And scraped both your knees!"

"Its fine, Johnny."

"Get inside right now and wash your wounds. I'll see if there's any antiseptic somewhere."

I go to the dingy bathroom on the second floor, next to his son's—Michael's—room. There's no electricity in the house but it's not that dark an afternoon, in spite of the looming clouds. I turn on the tap in the sink and let the water run for a while until it's not muddy any more. I hate using this bathroom. It stinks of stagnant water and is full of cobwebs and dust. I quickly wash my lips, knees and elbows that have cuts and scrapes on them.

I hear rustling sounds from Michael's room. I peek inside. Johnny has somehow managed to open a small box on Michael's study table and is fumbling to grasp a tube of ointment.

"I didn't know you could do that."

"Shhhh…this requires concentration."

I watch as the tube of what looks like Neosporin falls through his ghost like fingers again and again, the blue orb on his head glowing slightly brighter than usual. I watch transfixed. Why is he trying so hard? I can just go and grab the tube and save him the trouble. But he looks determined so I don't interfere.

The tube floats and falls. Floats and falls.

He finally gives up and looks at me disappointed. I walk to the table and pick up the tube.

"I'm sorry", he says flatly.

"It's ok. Thanks for finding it!" I say cheerfully as I start applying the ointment on my scrapes.

"You remind me of Michael. Thank you for coming by and talking to me so often."

"It's ok. I get bored at home anyway and I like talking to you too."

We both sit down on the floor together. The room is devoid of any furniture save for the dust covered table that somehow managed to survive whatever happened here.

"Hey Johnny, how come you never fall through the floor?"

He starts laughing and tells me that he has no idea. Sometimes, he tries to explain, he can run through walls and other times he just bangs into them soundlessly.

"Does it hurt?"

"No, everything is…numb. All the sounds are somewhat muted. Even the colours seem slightly paler. Getting used to walking without any sounds or feeling the ground was the scariest thing in the beginning. And now the scariest thing is knowing that you will go away some day and I won't have anyone to talk to."

"I'm not going away! I'll always be your friend!" I exclaim. "You're my best friend, Johnny. I don't have any other friends in class."

I start crying as I admit this. Johnny tries to put his arms around me to console me, but they pass right through.

"You should make friends with the cute girl sitting in front of you."

"What cute girl? I've told you her name a hundred times!" I sob.

"I know", he chuckles, "It's funny to see you blush when you say it.

SUSHMITA!"

"Shut up, Johnny", I giggle through my sobs.

"Why do you like her?"

"I don't know"

"Arrey, just think dikra[27] before saying you don't know. No more I-don't-knows from now on!"

I wipe away my tears and say nothing for a while. Johnny waits expectantly.

"She's very intelligent. And quiet."

"Just like you!"

I blush.

"What else do you like about her?"

"Hmmm…the way she talks. She's soft spoken and polite. And her Hindi is so much better than everyone else in the class."

"Have you ever called her on the phone?"

My eyes grow wide and I gulp. Johnny starts laughing.

"You have, haven't you?!"

"Yes, for homework stuff."

"Was your heart pounding hard when you called her?"

"Yes", I stammer.

"I miss that feeling. The blood rushing to your face when you call someone you love. The pounding of your heart. Your voice stammering on

---

[27] *Dikra*—Boy

the phone!"

I blush again because he used the word 'love'.

"What about the way she looks?"

"She's very pretty."

"The prettiest girl in the class?"

"Yes, I think so. Though the other guys think Sonakshi is the prettiest."

"Why do you think she's the prettiest then? Is it her hair? Her smile?"

"Yes, I like her smile. You can see her dimples. She always looks shy when she smiles. And I like her short brown hair."

"What about her body? Is she fit?"

"Her body?" I hesitate.

"Yeah, does she have nice boobs?"

"I don't know, I don't look at those things."

"What? When I was your age I would look at girls all the time! Girls with nice boobs and a small butt", Johnny giggled, "and then I would think about them at home when I was alone. Do you ever think about Sushmita when you're at home alone?"

My heart is pounding harder now and I start to sweat a little bit.

"It's ok to think about girls at your age. There's nothing wrong about it. All men think about women—that's how God meant it to be."

"Ok", I nod obediently.

"Ok, let's try that. You think about Sushmita and I'll think about my late missus."

"What?"

"It's going to be a fun game. Trust me. Now, think about Sushmita",

Johnny says.

I close my eyes. I think about the classroom. I see the back of Sushmita's head, the sunlight pouring through the leaves outside, making a beautiful pattern on her brown hair.

"Do you see her?"

"Yes", I say.

"Now imagine she is playing basketball with you. You like basketball, don't you?"

"Yes. But why basketball?" I ask.

"Arrey, because you like it and it's fun to imagine. Now…both of you are playing against each other. She's laughing and you're both having a great time playing."

I imagine the scene Johnny is describing. She's smiling and laughing with me. My heart feels light and fluttery. There are goose bumps all over my arms and legs. My wounds ache but in a strange and nice way. The air is slightly colder now. I open my eyes a little bit and find that Johnny is sitting behind me, his arms in front of me like he's trying to hold me.

"Close your eyes Jojo, and think about the basketball game you're playing with Sushmita. You're winning and she's only two points behind. It's her turn to shoot and she's dribbling the ball in front of you. She's sweating now and you can see she's wearing a white bra underneath her t-shirt. She makes a quick turn and trips over her feet. But you catch her! You are her hero! Both of you fall on the basketball floor. You're on top of her now. Doesn't it feel good? You're sweating and your sweat falls on her lips. You wipe it with your thumb."

I feel a dull ache in my underwear.

Johnny goes on, "She's looking at you now. She's waiting. You slowly start to pull her t-shirt up…"

I feel a sudden shudder run through me. The world goes completely blue for a second.

And then it's warm and yellow.

I see myself playing Lego with a young boy. It's my son, Michael. What a beautiful boy he is. The sunlight pouring through the leaves outside make a beautiful pattern on his soft brown hair. I've always loved that soft brown hair of his that his mother gave him. It smells of the sweet orange shampoo that he bathes with. I stroke his hair gently. He smiles at me. My heart feels light and fluttery. I take the small Lego car and run it over his left arm. He laughs softly.

"I love you, Michael."

He loves me too he replies with a smile. My eyes fill up with tears.

The ache in my underwear becomes more painful.

I kiss Michael's hands softly. Such tiny and beautiful hands he has. You're funny, baba, he laughs. I laugh with him.

"Shall we see how much you've grown, Michael?"

Shall I get the measuring tape from maman, he asks.

"No, I know another secret way", I lie to him. I only lie because I love him so much.

What secret way, he asks, his beautiful eyes growing wider, his soft lips turning into a smile.

"It's a secret! You can't tell maman. I will show you if you promise to keep it a secret."

Promise, he promptly replies.

"God promise?"

God promise, he promptly replies again.

"Good", I say. "We first need to take off our shirts for this", I say.

"You take her t-shirt off and see that she's only wearing a white bra underneath", a voice says from behind me.

Michael takes his shirt off. I see his ribs poking through his skin. I take my shirt off too. I feel the warm sunlight on my body.

I feel the coldness grow even colder around me and inside me. Are these my memories?

I put both my arms on his bony shoulders and run them from his shoulders to his neck and then back again. He giggles. I say I will need to measure him from behind now and move to sit behind him, his body sitting between my outstretched legs.

"She starts to unbuckle your belt", the voice says from another world.

I say I need to measure his nunu. Ok, he giggles. I tell him to undo his shorts and he does so obediently. What a beautiful boy he is. I undo my own pants.

I feel my shorts and underwear slide off.

"Oh, it's so small!" I exclaim as I hold his tiny penis in my left hand. Michael looks back at me with a worried look on his face. Is that bad, baba, he asks. "It's not good", I say. His worry manifests into a frown. I kiss him on his cheek and say, "I know a trick to make it bigger. Would you like me to teach you?" Yes, baba, he says almost in tears.

I feel something gently moving the skin on my penis up and down.

I feel him grow bigger in my left hand. I feel myself grow bigger in my right hand.

"You take her bra off. Her breasts are so big and soft. She keeps moving her hands on your nunu just like this, up and down, up and down…" the voice breathes into my ear.

I feel the up and down, up and down motion down below.

The door opens and Marlynn walks in.

The world goes blue again. I feel pins and needles on my face.

Why doesn't she understand how I feel about Michael? Doesn't she feel the same love for him that I feel? I just want to love him with all my heart. Is that so wrong? I am shaking and crying and begging with her to calm down but she doesn't want to understand.

I feel my chest tighten up. What is happening? Who is that lady? Is that my wife?

Who am I?

Marlynn is delirious. She tells me she knew all along. She knew I would do this to Michael. She knew I would, just like I did to the maid's boy. She knew and she didn't do anything. She knew and she didn't do anything. She knew and she didn't do anything she keeps screaming and sobbing.

The sunlight pouring through the leaves outside make a beautiful pattern on the kitchen knife as it trembles gently in her hands.

I feel hot tears running down my cheeks. Or are they Johnny's cheeks?

I wipe my tears and scream at her that Michael is different. Can't she see that the poor boy is crying now? Can't she see that the way I touched Michael was full of love and the way I touched the maid's dirty son was full of hatred?

Because I hate myself. Because I'm a worthless piece of shit. Isn't that why my father doesn't love me?

I'm begging Marlynn to put the knife down. She's sobbing uncontrollably now.

The knife glints in the sunlight briefly before the world becomes red.

The tears won't stop. I am sobbing for air as I lie exhausted on my side. My hand is cold and sticky. I've peed myself, all over my right hand. The pee is thick and white. My head feels heavy. My penis is throbbing. Why is my body so small again? Didn't it feel bigger and stronger just a moment ago? What time is it? Is dad worried about me?

I sit up and feel the whole room spin around me. I put my hand on the floor to keep myself from falling back down. But I pull it away at once because there's pee all over it, cold and sticky! And now the thick white pee is on the floor to the right of me and in front of me. I use my good hand to wipe my tears that won't stop pouring out. I keep clenching and unclenching my bad hand. Clenching and unclenching. Clenching and unclenching my cold and sticky hand.

Johnny is naked and sobbing in the corner too. I can barely see him because his blue orb of flame is almost transparent now. Why is he crying? Did I do something wrong? I don't understand.

"You looked inside! You looked inside me! You won't leave me like they did, will you? You won't go away now will you?" he manages through his sobs.

"No! You're my best friend, Johnny! You're my only friend!" I try to console him through my own sobs. What did I do? I didn't mean to look.

I didn't mean to look.

I DIDN'T MEAN TO LOOK.

I DIDN'T MEAN TO LOOK!

I DIDN'T MEAN TO LOOK!

I feel like something is squeezing my heart. The tears won't stop. There is no sunlight pouring through the leaves outside into the dark room. There are only clouds. Everything is darker now. The room is spinning again. Something happened here that I didn't understand. I did something bad today and I made Johnny cry. Am I a bad person? What did I just see? Was I not supposed to see? I can't breathe because I can't stop sobbing. The pins and needles on my face are coming back. My head feels heavy and my eyes are starting to sting. I see Michael's crying face as the knife plunges into his neck. I hear the crows of a thousand crows as I'm torn to pieces.

And just like that, the world goes black, as my consciousness and childhood decide to leave me at the same time.

25. Two Doors

I am sobbing uncontrollably. The forest is crying with me, the gloomy trees weeping dark green tears. The air is cold and stale.

Two doors open in front of me.

Behind the first door lies Megumi, naked on the bed, bathed in golden sunlight. Warm air flows through the door and wraps itself around me. I relish it. I realize that I am naked and shivering in the forest save for that bit of warmth.

Cold winds from the second door drive the warmth away. Behind it, I see the dark blue room where I was raped. Michael's room. I see a young boy lying catatonic. There's cold semen coagulating all around him on the floor. Johnny lies waiting in the dark corner of the room.

The first room is warm.

The second room is cold.

The first room promises love.

The second room promises only darkness.

The first promises to help me forget forever.

The second promises to never let me forget. Cold semen and rape await me there.

I look through the first door and see Megumi shaking my shoulder.

"Kiku, are you ok? Kiku, wake up", she says to me. I feel her warm touch on my shoulders.

I look through the second door and see the young boy lying on his side. There's a sea of cum around him now. Johnny is looking at him with feverish hunger in his eyes.

Shame, humiliation and hatred, the second room screams at me. All you need to do is shut the door, and it will be gone forever.

Warmth, love and numbness, the first room whispers to me. Step inside, and everything will go back to being normal.

Everything will go back to being the same.

Nothing will have to change.

And in that moment, the choice becomes clear to me.

Make your stand.

I walk to the first door. I feel its incredible warmth on my skin. I place my hand on the door handle...*Don't stop for anything*...and I close it.

My world becomes dark.

I then step through the second door to bring Jojo back.

26. Jojo

I'm sobbing on the bed. There's a naked boy besides me who is sobbing too. His back is facing me but I know who he is. I've always known.

Why did you leave me behind, Jojo sobs.

I wanted to forget you. I wanted to forget what Johnny did to you. What he did to us.

I have been alone for so long. I have been waiting for you all this time.

I know.

Do you hate me, Jojo asks.

I let out a loud cry. My heart feels like it's being squeezed into a tiny ball.

No, I don't hate you, Jojo. My body is shaking with every breath I manage to pull in. Trembling. Grieving.

Jojo turns to look at me. I see a frail young boy with neatly parted hair. I see the black stains of tear marks that have lined his cheeks for decades. How long have you been crying, Jojo? How many years' worth of tear stains are on your cheeks? I start to wipe them away. My thumbs start wiping the old stains away as new tears fall. Jojo starts wiping away the tears that are falling from my own eyes. Our eyes.

I hug Jojo tightly and tell him what I have always known to be true—I love you.

Something shifts inside me.

My heart expands. It becomes as large as my body, not a tiny ball any more. I see years of memories flood back inside me. I see the orphanage, I see Raju, I see Ganesh, I see Johnny, I see my father and for a brief moment, I see the face of my mother. I smell mint leaves.

Everything rushes in. I have made my stand.

My heart shrinks back to its normal size; the lingering feeling of largeness settles over the rest of me. Jojo and I are one again. I am Jojo and I am Kiku. One soul with two names. We have always been one. He has always been there for me. I have always been there for myself. And now I realize that.

I feel tear stains on my back. Megumi is crying too.

"Why are you crying?" I ask.

"I felt it. I felt you integrating", she manages through her tears as she hugs me tightly.

I feel her warmth spread all over me.

It's almost dawn when I finish telling Megumi the story of my childhood. The story of me, Jojo, Johnny. After the day that Johnny raped me, I never went back to that old mansion. I knew something bad had happened there and I tried to forget it. Guilt and shame became my primary emotions for a while. I started doing badly in school and would get into fights for no reasons. It was around that time that I was diagnosed with mild schizophrenia. My medication started at an early age. Guilt and shame were replaced with anger and numbness. It helped me forget a lot of things, even though traces of Jojo remained. When I moved to Singapore five years later, I changed my name to Kiku. Jojo needed to die for Kiku to start anew, or so I foolishly told myself.

"Somewhere inside me, it's still raining", Megumi had said to me about herself. Somewhere inside me, I'm still climbing over that gate covered in vines. I cannot escape what happened to me. I cannot undo what was done. None of us can. Instead, I accept it. I accept Jojo, for he is me. I love me, I accept me and I'll be there for me, forever. That is the promise I make to myself. And I intend to keep it.

After I finish, Megumi and I hold each other for what feels like an eternity.

She recites the haiku that she recited to me in Shiretoko—

"My home is empty

It waits for me to return

Even when I'm there"

My heart knows what it means.

"So what name should I call you now?" she asks me.

"It doesn't matter. Whatever you feel comfortable with. There's no difference between Jojo and Kiku."

"Then I prefer Kiku, if you don't mind."

"I don't mind", I smile.

Somewhere inside me, Jojo smiles too.

The room becomes colder. Bluer. Both of us feel it. We're suddenly aware of an old lady looking at us. She's wearing a yukata and has a blue flaming orb on top of her head. I've seen her before.

"Natsu ba-chan", Megumi gasps.

27. The Contract

"First name, Natsu. Last name, unknown. The perpetrator is living in a nearby village. Together with the aid of her partner, Jiji, Natsu has murdered the parents of several children over the years and kidnapped them. She and Jiji then raise these orphans as their own children, brainwashing them and using them to commit acts of terrorism throughout India. It's a highly organized operation which spans several states."

The man in black shows Ganesh a photograph of the woman. In the photograph the woman is reading a book to a child. Her face isn't clear but Ganesh can tell that she's wearing something Japanese.

"Is she Japanese?"

"Yes, we believe so. Both Jiji and Natsu are of Japanese descent and are believed to be former members of the Aum Shinrikyo cult that carried out terrorist attacks in Japan. Have you heard of the sarin gas attack that was carried out in the Tokyo subways in 1995?"

"It sounds familiar."

"The Aum Shinrikyo cult was responsible for that attack. We are not sure what Natsu and Jiji are doing in India but we do know that these are highly trained and dangerous individuals."

"And I'm supposed to kill them?"

"No. You're only supposed to eliminate Natsu. We have lost surveillance on the old man, Jiji."

"And if I do that, you will erase everything you have on me."

"No one can erase what you've done, Ganesh. Although we can exonerate you of all eleven crimes that you have committed."

"Can or will?"

"If you do your job, we will."

"I would like to see a contract."

The man in black starts laughing a manic laugh. His mouth is unusually large and his jaw seems like it has unhinged itself in the process of laughter.

"You want a fucking contract? You mean what, an assassination contract? Murderers don't make contracts, Ganesh. We only have our word. You murder people who commit petty crimes. I murder people who commit crimes against the country. But at the end of the day, we're both murderers. There can be no contract between us. Do you think such a thing would even hold up in the court of law? Are you stupid?

There is something that I can make with you though—a blood contract."

"A blood contract?"

"Yes, a contract made in blood."

"How do you make a blood contract?"

"We cut our palms and then we shake", the man in black says.

"I'll need my hands for the job", Ganesh says.

"As you wish."

"What do I do with the body?"

"We will handle the body. You focus on getting the job done."

Ganesh has been in the car for almost eight hours now. They haven't stopped once, not even for a toilet break. The car had driven into a dirt road a few hours ago when the sun had started to set. There are tall trees all around them. The black Mercedes swims through the sea of trees. The man in black asks him to put a black blindfold on. Ganesh does as he's told. He has no idea how this man has gathered all this intelligence on him. He knows everything. Right from Mr. Tripathi all the way to Mr. Gupta.

Ganesh feels the bumps in the road as the car trudges along. The crushing of the gravel changes to the crunching of leaves and twigs. The gentle rocking of the car puts him to sleep.

In his dream he sees crows. Thousands of them, looking at him silently, from the branches of trees, from the rooftops of farmhouses, on top of overturned buses, inside the living room of his home, on top of the bodies of his mother and father who have been neatly sown together into a blanket.

"Wake up."

He opens his eyes and yelps to see a giant crow sitting next to him.

"Wake up."

He opens his eyes to see the man in black sitting next to him with a leather bound box in his hands.

"What's that?" Ganesh asks as he rubs his eyes. The car is parked in the middle of a forest. The driver and the man in the front seat are nowhere to be seen.

The man in black gleefully opens the box. Inside, placed on a cushion of red velvet, is Ganesh's trusty bowie knife.

"I thought you'd like to use this."

Ganesh picks the knife up and tests its blade on the hair of his left arm. The hair falls off at the slightest touch of the blade. The knife has been sharpened incredibly well.

"Based on what our intelligence tells us, Natsu will come to the gates of the village at sunrise to remove the incense sticks that she burns in the evening. That would be your best time to strike. The gate is around one kilometre north of this location. After you have completed your tasks, head back here for extraction."

Ganesh and the man in black exit the car. He points Ganesh to the north and sends him on his way. The sky is a dark shade of blue. Daylight is probably still an hour away. Ganesh slowly makes his way through the forest, treading carefully. He takes a moment to relieve himself under a tree.

After walking for twenty minutes through the dark, Ganesh sees a large gate in the distance. It has two giant red pillars and a black arch on top. The gate looks very Japanese to him and he wonders where this village is even located in India. As he moves closer to the gates, he notices large ropes that are tied to the gate and that go through the trees. They have hollow paper squares attached to them.

Ganesh squats close to one of the gates, next to the rope. The incense sticks burning at the base of the gates smell nothing like the regular incense that he's used to smelling at home. The smoke has an oddly metallic smell to it, almost like blood. All of this feels like a dream. Any moment now, he's going to wake up in his bed, he thinks. The sky slowly starts turning orange. He hears the crunching of gravel. Someone is walking towards the gates. Ganesh sees the figure of an old woman through the bushes. She's dressed in a brown shawl like thing that he has seen Japanese people wear.

He hears a flute from somewhere far away.

"Every night in my dreams, I see you, I feel you..."

Where the hell is that music coming from?

The woman stops at the gate. She crouches down and begins to put out the incense stick. Ganesh begins to approach her, knife gleaming in right hand.

"Far across the distance, and spaces between us..."

She hears the rustling of the leaves and starts to turn around. Ganesh jumps out from the bushes and plunges the knife in her back. She lets out a scream. Ganesh grabs her left shoulder, pulls the knife out and stabs her again. And again.

"Once more you open the door..."

The woman falls over. There is blood pooling on the ground—hot, steaming blood. He grabs her and turns her around. The old woman is grasping for his arm. What does she want? Ganesh raises his knife high in the air and prepares to plunge it into her heart with both his hands. He's feverish with excitement. Oh what a beautiful carpet I will make with your skin, he thinks!

"Come forth", Natsu says.

Ganesh feels sick. He sees the creepy man from the bus who has a buffalo horn sticking out of his throat, his eyes glowing blue. He sees himself plunging the knife into the throat of a young girl and decapitating her with the force of it. He sees himself murdering family after family of innocent people. 32 families in 16 cities. He sees himself manically laughing. He sees raincoats and newspaper articles and sewing kits and meat grinders and totem poles made of flesh and bones.

He sees the bloody mess of the old woman underneath him whose blood is spreading everywhere, boiling, steaming, scalding his hands.

"We need to finish her", Omkara screams.

"I am making my stand", Ganesh replies.

He drops the knife, screaming, and begins to vomit.

He feels a great darkness coming out of his body. Out it comes through his throat, boiling up his insides, burning his oesophagus. He vomits out a flaming blue orb and then a hand and then an arm and then his jaw unhinges and an entire man comes out of him.

Ganesh's jaw hangs swaying in the air. He feels like an empty shell, ready to be blown away at the slightest gust of wind. He sees a man with a flaming blue orb on top of his head. He sees the creepy man from the bus who flew into his mouth and had been living inside his body for the past twenty years. He sees the old lady's body whom he had just murdered in cold blood, without any question, to absolve himself of what that man from the bus had done. What he himself had done. The old lady's spirit rises from her body. She walks up calmly to the bus man and put her hands on the flaming blue orb on top of him.

"The village isn’t meant for you", she declares.

"What are you doing?" Omkara screams.

With one swift motion, she crushes his orb. There’s an explosion of blue light through the forest. Ganesh is blinded by the light, his retinas permanently damaged by its brilliance. He has made his final stand. He collapses to the floor and is finally able to let go of his spirit, forever.

28. Yuki

Yuki came to the village of Tochuu when she was four. Old Jiji had found her lying next to the body of her father, talking to his Aoirei. He had been stabbed fatally in a robbery and died on the outskirts of a small town. Yuki talked to him as if he were still alive. The father kept urging her to go search for help and leave him be, but Yuki had refused to budge. She had always been a stubborn one. Jiji ended up bringing both Yuki and the father back to Tochuu, the girl refusing to leave her father's side.

Natsu fell in love with the girl at first sight. She had soft brown hair and inky blue eyes that were full of determination. You could tell from one look that Yuki would one day grow up to become a fierce and beautiful woman. The other Aoirei in the village were quite taken too by this blue-eyed girl who had accompanied her deceased father to this place outside of time. Father and daughter lived peacefully for a while in the village.

Soon the day came for her father to go. "Yuki-chan, I have fulfilled my purpose", her father had tried to explain at the mouth of the Well of Memories where all Aoirei must make their final journey. The other Aoirei looked on, knowing that they too would have to make that journey one day, when they were ready.

"Jiji-san will take care of you. He will teach you how to be a Guardian. I can see it in you, Yuki-chan, your fiery spirit glows bright."

"I want to go with you", she said, tears welling up in her inky blue eyes.

Her father knelt down to hug her. In a flash, Yuki saw her father's entire life and she understood.

"Goodbye, father", she said, tears streaming down her face.

Jiji realized early on that Yuki was different from the other Guardians that had come and gone through Tochuu. She had the unique ability of experiencing an Aoirei's life by letting them enter her. "Scrying", she used to call it. She could use her abilities—depending on her mood—to help the

Aoirei who had forgotten the realizations that had led them to Tochuu in the first place. Jiji forbade her from using her abilities when she was younger, for fear of traumatizing her. But as she grew into an increasingly rebellious and beautiful girl, she would sneak away and try to help the Aoirei lost in the forest on her own. Yuki loved the Forgotten Forest more than she liked living in Tochuu and would often not come back until just before sunset—which was the time for the crows to hunt. By the time she was an adult, she had figured out a way to go back and forth between the world of Tochuu and world of mortals, much like Jiji himself and the Guides.

The Guides were meant to live outside the village and to guide the Aoirei there.

Guardians like Natsu and Yuki were meant to stay inside the village, to protect it.

That was the way.

Old Jiji fulfilled several roles, including that of being the disciplinarian.

Jiji wasn't the least bit happy about having a Guardian pop in and out of the realm of Tochuu at her own convenience. Passing through the forest to cross over was always a dangerous affair, no matter how many times you had done it. Then came the complexity of ending up in the wrong time, both while leaving and returning. Time doesn't flow straight in either realm. Its turbulence only becomes more obvious the more you travel back and forth. Things that belonged in the past ended up with things that belonged in the future. Inexperienced Guides would sometimes end up in the wrong time after guiding their quarry. Jiji would have to search for them and bring them back, which was always a hassle.

He tried to explain all of these things to Yuki. When explanations failed, he would punish her. The more he tried to control her though, the more she would rebel. When they had really bad arguments, she would vanish into the forest for days, presumably back in the mortal world—because nothing could survive the Karasu in the forest between the hours of sunset and sunrise. Night was their time. It was The Master's time.

Natsu tried to inculcate "womanly" values in Yuki, like a mother would to a daughter. Yuki would listen, nod dutifully to her mother and then do the exact opposite. She would go and disturb the forest's caretakers, the Aoirei who tended to the forest's needs. She would climb trees, amass an army of pet frogs and go on "hunting expeditions" with them, smuggle cigarettes into the forest and smoke them while reading manga. Natsu had no idea where she got these things from but it was evident that Yuki could juggle multiple lives, in and out of Tochuu. The more Yuki scryed with the Aoirei, the more she learnt about the outside world and was enamoured by it. The Aoirei would tell her amazing stories—stories of war, love, travel, knowledge. And family. Those Aoirei who were not ready to make the journey to the Well of Memories would ask her to find out if their families were doing fine. Yuki wasn't stupid and she knew that entertaining such requests would only take them farther away from the truth that was inside the well. In those moments, mother and daughter would really shine, working together to bring those Aoirei back to the path of completeness. Any time an Aoirei regressed by yearning for the life they once had, Yuki and Natsu would step in to bring them back. Many of these Aoirei, after their talks with mother and daughter, would choose to make their journey to the well.

The Well of Memories stood in the middle of Tochuu. As a child, Yuki would sometimes run all the way around its large circumference, again and again. The well was an anomaly to her. Some days she would complete the circle faster and some days it would take almost forever to complete a single round. It was as if the well could expand and contract in diameter. The spiralling stone steps leading to its bottom (if it had a bottom, Yuki wondered) made her feel dizzy if she looked at them for too long. Jiji had said to her—

"You must never go down those steps Yuki-chan. That journey is only meant for the Aoirei, and not for human beings. We are not ready to face the truth about our lives. Most humans aren't. We are too attached to our body. Our senses. Our breath. We are not ready to face a truth that is bigger than ourselves."

That was one of the very few things Yuki had actually listened to.

Until she was twenty nine years old.

One day, twenty nine year old Yuki came back and locked herself up in the small shed she had claimed as her home. Seeing Jiji and Natsu day in and day out made her head hurt, so she had found a place where she could be by herself. She refused to talk to anyone, including the Aoirei. This was certainly unusual because the Aoirei were her best friends and even when she had had altercations with Jiji (always Jiji and seldom Natsu) she would always find a comforting ear among the blue spirits who loved her dearly. After seven days of silence she finally confessed to Jiji—"I'm pregnant. Don't ask me how and why. It just happened ok?"

Jiji was silent.

Yuki asked him, "You have nothing to say?"

"You told me not to ask."

"That's right."

"What will you do with the child?"

"What do you mean what will I do? I will raise it of course. Him. Or her."

"On your own?"

"Yes, on my own. The father of the child doesn't know. And I don't intend to tell him."

"Natsu and I will help you."

"I didn't ask for your help. I just came to tell you."

Jiji was surprisingly calm and this bothered Yuki. Where was the anger? She had prepared herself for an argument and Jiji was being nice instead. Confused by his affection, Yuki locked herself up for another two days for good measure and devoted her time to the single-minded task of crying. On the second night, she heard a strange sound coming from the well. She opened the door to her shed to listen more closely. It was a rhythmic humming. The air was cold, so Yuki wrapped herself in a thick woollen shawl that Natsu had made for her. Yuki walked silently through the village. The Aoirei kept to a humanly schedule and were fast asleep, their blue lights leaking through the nooks and crannies of their wooden homes. The sound got clearer as she approached the well. The sky was full of stars and luckily there was a full moon to guide her without the use of a torch. She approached the perimeter of the well and peeked inside. Moonlight poured into its mouth, disappearing into the inky blackness. She could feel the humming on her skin now, vibrating, pulsing. Her belly felt queasy. She hadn't eaten all day. The humming sound mixed with the rumbling of her stomach.

She looked around to see if Jiji had been watching her from the shadows. She always did that before doing something Jiji would disapprove of.

The well had a shallow wall. You could climb onto its thick edge without needing any support if you were agile enough. Looking down though, into its never-ending mouth could make anyone feel dizzy. Yuki climbed down its spiralling steps, one hand always on the cold and dry wall of the well, the other floating in the air. The steps were cold underneath her feet, worn and uneven. She had to descend slowly.

The humming resonated inside her. She could feel it slowly increasing in intensity as she went further down. The moonlight faded away after a while and all that remained was darkness. Yuki neither looked up, nor looked down. She closed her eyes and kept descending—further and further down, her hands and feet guiding her along. The air went from being fresh and crisp to dank and musty. The dryness of the walls gave way to sliminess and mould. Her fingers flinched at the wetness. The steps became slippery and she had to be cautious, stepping sideways sometimes. Her floating hand felt the air getting heavier. She could feel it between her fingers, almost liquid in texture. It felt warm, like she had run a bath which was exactly the same temperature as her body's. She started to enjoy the sensation. After a while it felt as if her whole body was floating. She glided down the steps with ease. She kept gliding and gliding for hours, maybe days, maybe months. Who could even tell? The humming had disappeared a long time ago.

Skipping, floating, swimming through the well, Yuki went deeper and deeper and deeper.

It started getting warmer. Warmer and warmer and warmer. Until it was boiling hot. Sweat flowed from her body. Her blood boiled. She swam in her own sweat.

Struggling, drowning, paddling through the well, Yuki went deeper and deeper and deeper and deeper.

The blood inside her belly boiled and steamed with rage. She was filled with fear and anger, anger and fear. Her belly bubbled, the skin popping and forming, popping and forming. Her insides cried. She saw the child inside her being boiled alive. Yuki screamed. She screamed for the child. The child screamed for her, inside her boiling insides. Amidst the screaming and boiling and popping and forming, Yuki realized that she was running on solid ground.

The screaming stopped. The world was cold again.

She had reached the bottom. She opened her eyes and saw nothing but darkness. She looked up and saw a tiny dot of blue. What was up and what was down anyway?

Suddenly, there was a flash of light.

Yuki screamed at its brightness. The light burned her eyes. She had to close them, cover them with her hands, kneel and crouch so that her body could block it. The light still made her eyes hurt.

"Yuki", the light said.

Yuki replied with the groans and complaints one makes when suddenly woken up from a good dream. She curled up into a ball and stayed like that for some time. Her closed eyes slowly adjusted to the light.

"Open your eyes, Yuki", the light commanded her gently.

Yuki opened her eyes slowly. The walls of the well were far away from her. Yuki realized that the well had grown wider and wider as she had climbed down its steps, like a cone. Above her, where she had seen a dot of blue, were millions of blue orbs, floating silently like fireflies. Some were big, some were small, but together they felt like an entire universe of blue stars. Only one light was different than the others, the one that stood a few feet away from her. This light was brighter, a warmer shade of blue. It stood tall and vertical, almost in the shape of a man. Blue light ebbed and flowed from it and enveloped everything it touched in its warm blueness.

"Why are you here, Yuki?" the light asked.

"I don't know."

"Everyone who comes here knows why they are here."

"But I don't."

"What brought you here?"

"The humming sound."

"Where is the sound now?"

"I don't hear it any more."

"Listen closely", the light said.

Yuki closed her eyes and listened. She heard nothing at first. Then she heard her breath. Her heartbeat. And in her abdomen, she heard the hum again. Soft and soothing.

"It is inside me", Yuki said.

"Inside you", the light repeated.

"I came here because of what's inside me."

"Yes."

"I saw him being boiled inside me."

"Your blood boils with fire. Guardian blood runs through your veins. Do you remember your blood rites?"

"Yes, I do. Jiji taught me. It would keep the Karasu away, he had told me."

"And it will kill the son inside you."

"The son inside me", Yuki repeated in a trance.

"You are bound to your rites, Yuki", the light said.

"Then unbind me."

"The crows will hunt you. Your blood protects you."

"But it will destroy my child."

"Yes, your blood will destroy him. His body, to be precise."

"Then unbind me."

The light was silent.

"I want him to live, so unbind me", Yuki shouted.

"Do you realize who his father is?"

"Why does it matter?"

"Everything matters", the light replied.

"Please, just unbind me so that my son may live."

"Remember your blood rites."

Yuki recited her blood rites without missing a word—

"I am the Guardian of the lost,

My blood boils with the fire in my soul,

Blue it blazes, like rain falling on scorched earth,

I bind my steaming blood to myself."

"And now I unbind you", the light added.

Yuki felt her whole body grow cold, like life itself had been drained out of her. She collapsed on the ground.

"I unbind you of your blood and give you the light instead.

You are a Guardian no more.

Not to yourself.

Not to the lost.

Not to your son.

He will have two names and two souls. One soul will have two names and one soul will have none. Two souls and two names.

He will live a life of pain and numbness, numbness and pain.

He will lose everything.

And once he has lost everything, you will be his Guardian again."

Yuki fell into a deep and dreamless sleep.

Rap, rap, rap.

Rap, rap, rap, the door said. Yuki woke up in her shed. Jiji was having a fit outside, knocking incessantly with his wooden staff.

"I don't care what you want, Yuki-chan! Natsu and I will help you with your child. Wake up!" he was shouting.

Yuki woke up and touched her belly. It felt warm while the rest of her body felt cold. She yawned and stretched herself. Jiji kept shouting outside and it made her smile. She wondered how he would react if he she opened the door and planted a big wet kiss on him. The thought made her laugh. She then opened the door and did exactly that.

29. Tochuu

I've been here before. I recognize the wooden houses. I recognize the grassy paths and the blooming flowers. I recognize the tall red torii gates that I used to run through and then past the rose bushes. I recognize the giant well in the centre of the village.

Hundreds of people gather near it. The crowd is a mixture of human beings and Aoirei. These are all the other Guides, Megumi and I realize. We are all dressed in black, the Aoirei dressed perpetually in grey. The old man known as Jiji (I remember bits and pieces of him too) is at the centre of the makeshift gathering. There is a table in front of him, atop which rests, covered in white cloth, the body of Natsu ba-chan. We used to make hollow paper squares for the ropes together.

"The crows have struck", the old man addresses the crowd in English.

"They found a human assassin to kill your mother, the last Guardian to The Village of Lost Souls. I have no doubt that they will attack us when night falls."

There are murmurs in the crowd. I can feel the anger all around me.

"We must realize what's at stake here. We are the light that shines bright in the darkest hour of the night. We are the final destination for the lost. Without us, there will be no truth. We must protect Tochuu at all costs. We must protect it with our lives. And when that life ends, we must protect it with whatever comes after that. We must fight!"

The crowd cheers him on. I join in reluctantly at first but all the energy around me makes me join in earnest.

Jiji starts calling out names and assigns them different roles. Some are sent to protect the gates. Some are tasked to bury the body of Natsu ba-chan. Some oversee bringing back weapons from the mortal world. Megumi and a group of Guides are put in charge of protecting the well. I am not assigned a role.

Megumi is flocked by a group of people and Aoirei. I don't want to bother her so I decide to walk around the village by myself. Everyone here is moving with purpose, except for me. I watch as a group of men and women lift up Natsu ba-chan's body and carry it through the grassy streets. A large group of Aoirei follow them, grieving her passing. Natsu ba-chan's Aoirei is nowhere to be seen. Come to think of it, shouldn't Jin be around here somewhere?

I stop one of the passing Aoirei to ask if he's seen a young boy, maybe seven years old. The man tells me there haven't been any children in Tochuu for a while. Children usually don't become Aoirei he tells me but he's not sure. Maybe the boy I'm looking for went into the Well of Memories he says.

"But I was with him a few days ago."

"Time works differently here, young man. You should know that. Are you a new Guide? Maybe you guided him to the past?"

It's possible I think. He might've gone to the past and made his journey to the well. Megumi did say she saw a younger Natsu ba-chan when she brought Jin here.

"What is in the well?"

"The Well of Memories? No one knows what's inside. Some call it the truth. Some call it the end. It's the place where you must make your final journey, if you have the courage to come face to face with your own life. I've heard there are other places like this, but I only know of Tochuu. I'm worried it's too late for me now. I waited too long and now the crows will come for me."

The man begins to cry grey tears and walks away.

Have I come face to face with my own life?

Dark clouds cover the sky, as if in anticipation for what's about to come. I look at my watch and the dials look all bent and warped out of shape. It's time-to-get-fucked o'clock, my watch says.

While wandering aimlessly, I come across a small plot of land through the trees where they are burying Natsu ba-chan. They have dug a grave for her and are lowering her body inside using ropes. I can see that there's another grave right next to hers which has a headstone marking it. I can't read the name on it from here.

"Kiku", Megumi calls me from behind.

I turn to face her. We stand and stare at each other. She's dressed in a black suit. I'm dressed in my own black suit that I bought with her. She's holding two axes in her hands. She walks up to me.

"Kiku, this might not be your fight. Natsu ba-chan raised me as her own, so I fight for her. I think a lot of the Guides here feel that way too and so we choose to fight. I can show you the way out, but I must stay behind."

Thunder rumbles somewhere in the distance. The breeze turns into a gust and brings with it the smell of rain.

"Do you want me to leave?" I ask.

"I want you to make your own choice."

"You didn't answer my question."

Megumi looks straight into my eyes and replies, "No, I don't want you to leave."

I extend my arm to her. She hands me one of the axes.

"I've been here before Megumi. I'm connected to this place. I want to fight for it, even though I don't fully understand why. The answer is within me. I can't grasp it yet, but I feel it there.

I don't know a lot of things, but I do know this—I made my choice the day I met you.

I choose to fight by your side."

Lightning cracks dramatically in the dark sky. We both giggle and then we smile. We hug each other harder than we've ever hugged before. If there ever was such a thing as the perfect hug, then this was it. Our bodies convey the love our words cannot. I choose to die by your side, we say to each other. I choose to stand with you, we say.

We walk back to the Well of Memories, hand in hand, axes in our other hands.

There are others gathered there, each with a weapon of their own. There are guns, katanas, more axes, maces and even crossbows. Snipers are setting up on top of some of the wooden houses. Jiji is walking from place to place with a wooden staff, talking to people, checking the weapons. Some Aoirei stand with the living. Others hide inside their wooden homes.

"What happens now?" I ask.

"We wait for sunset", Megumi replies.

"And then?"

"And then we fight the Karasu. We fight the Master."

I look around me again. These are all regular people. Some might be bakers and bankers and software engineers. How many of us are trained to fight, I wonder.

Wind howls through the forest as we wait for sunset. A light rain begins to fall. Everyone has picked a place in the village where they will make their stand. Nobody moves. The air feels electric.

"How exactly do we know when the sun has set? The sky is covered in clouds."

"Oh, you'll kn…"

Everyone shuts up at once. I hear crowing in the distance. It doesn't sound like a lot at first, but soon the sky is filled with their cacophony. The rain gets heavier.

"GET READY", shouts Jiji.

The crowing grows louder. And suddenly, the sound of gunfire and screams fill the air.

"AIM AT THE SKY!"

I see a fluid, shimmering darkness approaching. Thousands of large black birds are descending from the sky, along with the rain.

People are firing frantically in the air. Dark blobs are landing and crushing people into pink mist underneath them. Sharp black beaks are tearing flesh from bone.

Death rains upon us.

A black feathered creature lands in front of Megumi and me. Megumi lets out a roar and charges it with her axe. It pushes her aside with a blow from its arm. I let out a shout of my own and manage to land my axe on its shoulder. An unearthly scream pierces my ears. Sharp black talons kick me square in the chest, ripping my skin off. I get launched into the air. My back, instead of finding solid ground, finds thin air. I fall into the Well of Memories.

30. The Well of Memories

"Jojo. Jojo. Wake up Jojo."

My mother is sitting beside me on the bed, running her hand through my hair, her beautiful blue eyes staring at me.

"We're going to Tokyo today. Come on, get ready."

I yawn and stretch my arms out. She hugs me and makes me sit up. I love being woken up like this. I don't like alarms. They're stupid and noisy and scare me. I bring my stool with me to the bathroom sink, climb up and brush my teeth.

Mom is preparing breakfast. I like to eat cornflakes and milk for breakfast, with a spoon full of strawberry jam mixed in. We finish eating by 9:30am. Our train is at 10:24am. We had already packed our bags to leave the night before. Mom likes being punctual.

"You must always be on time, lest you want to end up in a different time", she would always say.

We reach the railway station half an hour early. I want to buy some snacks for the train ride. Mom knows I love sandwiches so she buys me my favourite—katsu sando. We head upstairs to the platform. The platform is crowded.

She holds my hand. I squeeze her warm hand and her warm hand squeezes back.

The air around us is cold and I see my breath come out in puffs of white in front of me. I'm tapping my feet to the tune of a song in my head. My mother is amused by my tapping and asks me what song I'm thinking about.

"Laaaast Christmas, I gave you my heart", I sing.

She starts laughing and then sings along. We sing until we can't remember the words to the song any more.

"Can I eat my sandwich now?"

"We'll eat it in the train, or else you'll get hungry again", she tells me.

"Fine", I pout.

She squeezes my cheek and I giggle.

"Jojo", someone calls me from behind.

I turn to look behind me and the world goes still. Natsu ba-chan is standing behind me. There's a blue orb of flame on top of her head. She's wearing a grey yukata. Her clothes have no colour, much like the rest of her. Everything about her is a shade of grey, save for the pale blue flame. She's smiling at me. Her smile is benevolent and it fills me with a feeling of warmth. I smile back at her and wave.

"Jojo, how have you been doing?"

"I'm good oba-chan. How are you?"

"I've had better days", she laughs. "How is Yuki-chan doing?"

"Mom is great too", I say beaming.

"Listen Jojo, there is something important you must do. Something very very important. You must not forget to do it when the time comes. You must make your stand. And you must let the light out. Do you understand Jojo? When the time comes, you must make your stand and let the light out."

CAW!

I open my eyes. My head is aching. I touch it and it's wet. I look at the palm of my hand and it's black in the blue light. I'm bleeding. The Karasu are in front of me. There are five of them, maybe six. I can't tell because my head is spinning. They are all looking at me but not moving.

"Jojo", I hear a voice call out my name from behind them. The Karasu move to either side of the voice. A dark figure emerges. It's the thing that chased me in the forest. It has the face of Johnny and razor sharp black teeth. I can barely make out a black smoky orb floating on top of his head. His black feathers are shimmering in the blue light all around us. I realize that I'm at the bottom of the well. I look up to see a universe of blue stars. Or are they souls? A column of water falls somewhere far away. The well is enormous and I'm not at the centre of it where the rain is falling.

"You have finally returned, Jojo. Did you miss me?"

"Who are you?"

He laughs a manic laughter. His eyes are hollow and black liquid pours out of the sockets like tears.

"I am, what people call 'The Master'. Some call me The Darkness. Some call me The Hollow."

Behind him, I see other Guides and Aoirei who have fallen into the well, fighting, being torn apart. Blue lights being swallowed whole. Their screams seem distant and muffled.

"Pay them no heed. This is between us. Kazama is nowhere to be found. Maybe you can bring him back. Do you remember what I did to your mother, Jojo? Do you remember how fiercely she fought for you?"

I hear the flapping of a thousand wings. Dark wings, flapping all around me.

"Do you hear Yuki screaming?"

I hear the screams of the Guides. I look at the floor. There's an axe at my feet. Megumi's axe. I pick it up.

"Maybe I should give you a reminder of what I did to her soft flesh, Jojo."

A sudden and violent anger guides me to the Karasu closest to me. I land my axe square in the middle of its head and split it in two. The one behind it tries to kick me but I block it with the body of Karasu I axed. The others start closing in. I swing my axe and catch one of them in the arm. It punches me in the chest and sends me flying to the ground. The air is knocked out of me and I'm ready to throw up. I take a few deep breaths and stand up again, my ribs probably fractured, my chest heaving with pain. I don't have my axe. It's lodged in one of the ten arms. Ten arms and five sharp beaks approach me. One of them flaps their wings and jumps high. While I'm distracted by it, another one charges me and knocks me to the ground. The one that jumped, lands on both my arms. I hear a cracking sound. Just as it's about to peck my face clean off, a mace lands on top of its head and splits it open like a black watermelon.

Megumi saves me yet again.

One of the Karasu pecks her hard on the back. Blood spurts in an arc as she falls on top of me.

I look up at Megumi. Megumi looks at me.

She smiles her deep dimpled smile.

"Remember our promise, Kiku", she says.

She hugs my head and pushes me to the ground, pinning my body with her own.

Don't do this, Megumi.

The Karasu close in.

"DON'T DO THIS!"

After that, all I hear are her screams and my own.

31. Mother

Mom and I are making paper squares in the village. 'Shide', they are called. We will hang them on the 'shimenawa' ropes later. Natsu ba-chan is out hunting for dinner.

I have made twenty shide today! The 'Aoirei' (I have trouble saying it)...the blue people love my paper squares. I wanted to use coloured paper but mom told me we must use white. It will ward off the bad spirits she tells me, and let the good ones inside. Every few months, we go into the forest and replace the old shide with the new ones.

"It's late Jojo. We will go in only for a short time, ok? We don't have to hang all of them today."

"Ok", I say. But I have made twenty of them. Twenty perfect ones. I have never made so many before.

We walk through the bushes and into the sea of trees. I stay close to my mother because she knows every inch of the forest. I see squirrels and birds playing in the trees. The trees are so tall. The sky above them is beautiful. I can see the stars already.

We come to the rope. Mom starts unfastening one of the old shide strips and I hand her a brand new one to fasten. We walk to the next strip, which is farther away. I keep looking up at the trees and the beautiful sky.

Starlight winks through the leaves.

My foot gets caught in an overgrown root and I trip. My shide strips fall all over the ground. Mom is walking ahead. I better collect everything before she sees that I've dropped everything on the floor and made them dirty. I pick them up one by one, brushing the dirt off them, counting…eleven, twelve, thirteen…

"Hey", someone whispers.

There's a man on the other side of the rope.

"You missed one", he says, pointing to one of the square strips that has landed near his feet. He has strange feet.

"Thank you", I say as I cross underneath the rope and go towards the strip he's pointing to.

"You're welcome, Jojo", he says and starts laughing.

"JOJO", I hear my mother scream. I turn to see her running towards me.

The man starts laughing like a madman. He's covered in black feathers. His feet have black claws on them. My mother jumps on top of me and starts screaming. Why is she screaming? I feel like something is pounding on her back. The man is hitting her! He is laughing. She is screaming. My mother keeps screaming for Jiji. Jiji, Jiji she keeps on screaming. I see blood running down the side of her face. The madman is ripping her back with his claws. Other black claws land all around us and start clawing my mother. WHY ARE THEY DOING THIS? SOMEONE HELP US!

My mother's screams are interspersed with the sounds of flapping wings.

Dark wings, flapping all around us.

Flapping.

Cawing.

Biting.

Tearing.

I hear Jiji screaming.

"JIJI", I scream.

My mother's face is covered in blood and tears.

I hear the sound of clothes tearing. The sound of crows laughing.

She has stopped screaming. I don't want her to die. I don't want her to die. I DON'T WANT HER TO DIE.

Her blood falls into my eyes. It keeps falling and falling and falling, like a river. I am blinded by it. The smell of mint leaves from my mother's hair is mixed with the metallic smell of blood. I keep screaming and screaming and screaming. Her blood fills my mouth. I only see red and red and red. And then I feel an incredible warmth enter my body. The feeling lasts only for a moment and then her body becomes as cold as ice. The claws keep pounding away at her ice cold body. I hear the thwacks of a wooden staff. I close my eyes and want to die.

32. White and Blue

I open my eyes. Megumi's body is lying motionless on top of mine. I hear the thwacks of a wooden staff. I roll her over. Her eyes are closed. I touch her face. I can't feel my arms or my fingers.

"Hey, wake up", I ask her.

She doesn't want to wake up.

"Oye, Megumi."

Teardrops fall on her cheeks. Drip-drop. She doesn't flinch.

Maple leaves fall all around us.

I hear a scream nearby. Old Jiji has been impaled by the Master's right hand. His staff drops to the floor.

"Goodbye, old friend", the Master says.

The Master extinguishes yet another life that held importance to me. I shake Megumi again with my arms that don't feel anything.

"Wake up, Megumi!"

"Wake up!"

"Wake up!"

Megumi lies still. I place my head on her chest. Her heart does not beat. Her eyes remain closed.

I close my own eyes and I see her face half buried in a pillow, a single brown eye looking straight at me. She closes her eye.

I see her floating into a star-filled sky on a forgotten island. The island I had promised to take her to. I reach out to grab her, but she floats away—higher and higher. Until she is gone.

I have now lost everything.

My body begins to shake. Something inside me wants to come out. It starts at my belly and makes its way up to my chest. My chest feels like it's about to burst from the inside, throbbing, vibrating, as if it cages a thousand angry bees. Blue light starts pouring out through my ribs, my broken bones, my broken arms. All at once, everything explodes in a deafening roar.

I let the light out.

My heart bursts with anger and my mouth quivers from the sounds emanating from deep within me. These are the primal and terrifying cries of my soul.

Everything turns blue.

I keep screaming and screaming. With every second of my scream, the world becomes clearer and clearer. The blackness that was once there, turns into blue. And the blue starts turning into white.

My anger is white hot.

I see crows. Not Karasu, but ordinary crows. They crow and scream and caw and claw at blue orbs, trying to become whole again, screaming for the souls they once had. I feel their desperation. My body moves on its own as it glides from one crow to the next and relieves them of their sorrow. With swift motions of my wrist, I twist and I twist and I twist. I twist their necks to end their hollow lives that have only seen apathy and agony.

I twist and twist and twist and twist. I take a moment to look at my hands that are covered in blood and feathers. Blue light burns through them with the ferocity of my soul as they rip their way through the crows, one by one, all the way to the one they call Master.

"You woke up", the Master crows.

I reply with a deeper roar, acknowledging his statement. Flaming hands make a blue arc through the air. Skin meets feather. Soul meets body. The world shatters.

33. Kazama

A long time ago, there was a man named Kazama. Kazama had been digging the deepest well in the world for over four years. He was one of the thousands that the Emperor had imprisoned to build him a "Gateway to Hell". The Emperor was not a wise ruler, according to Kazama, and had foolishly chosen to believe the words of soothsayers and charlatans who claimed that there was a greater purpose to all of this. By meeting, Yama, the God of Death himself, he would supposedly barter a trade to become an immortal being. Now that the well was almost complete, the Emperor himself, and his council of fools, had come to inspect it and to make preparations for whatever ceremonies were required to summon Yama.

Kazama had other plans though. Over the last year, he had been orchestrating a daring escape from the clutches of the Emperor. With the aid of his comrades, he planned to take the emperor hostage and free all the prisoners.

The crux of his plan lay in the art of stealth. And Kazama was a master of stealth. Before he was imprisoned, Kazama was one of the most wanted thieves in the land. He would steal for the thrill of it. It was as if his body would move of its own accord and bring him along for the ride. Kazama didn't steal from the poor though, for he himself had grown up in poverty and understood the daily struggle for survival. Where each day was lived to the fullest because sometimes there wasn't a second day in sight.

Kazama's right-hand man, Jichirou, handed him a map of the royal camp. Jichirou, was most resourceful in recruiting people for a greater cause. That was his talent. He had made friends with the prison guards long before Kazama had confided in him his bold plan. Through the guards, and through the friends of the guards, and through the children of the friends of the guards, and a complex network of informants, Jichirou had managed to recreate a very detailed schedule of guard duties, supply tents, camp layouts—any information that might be of help to Kazama.

Kazama's left-hand man, Shinji, though not as intelligent as Jichirou, was well loved by the prisoners for his hard work and kindness. Shinji was in charge of creating the escape route for Kazama. For the plan to work, Kazama would first have to find a way out of the prison camp in which everyone was held. This was the hardest part, because the prison camp was heavily guarded.

"Are you sure you can distract them long enough, Jiji?" Kazama asked.

"Of course", replied Jichirou, mysterious as always. He never revealed why he was imprisoned, but Kazama assumed he must've been a minister or high ranking official in his life before imprisonment.

"The tunnel is ready", Shinji added.

The three men bowed to each other and set off in opposite directions. Shinji had employed some of his comrades to dig a hole through the latrines that would lead to the world beyond the prison walls. No one else dared to escape, for even if they did, the woods surrounding them were full of soldiers and noisy crows. On the far side of the prison, Kazama heard shouting and commotion. That was surely the work of Jichirou. He hid patiently as the guards posted near the latrines started walking over to the other side to see what the clamour was about. Seeing his chance, Kazama crept quietly into the latrine and dove head first into the muck underneath.

Digging his way through the shit, for what seemed like an eternity, he emerged on the other side of the wall. The hardest part was complete. Slipping through the soldiers patrolling the forest was a simple task for Kazama's body. It crouched and slithered through the bushes, always aware of what was around it. From time to time, he would look up at the stars to guide him in the right direction. The royal camp was several miles south of where the prison and the "Gateway to Hell" was. Along the way, he quietly washed the shit off him in a stream of water. The crows watched him bathe silently. He silently bowed to them as a way of gratitude and set off again.

Jichirou had mapped out exactly where the royal guard stored their supplies. He slipped into one of these stores and stole himself a battered old uniform. Even after wearing it, Kazama was careful to avoid routes which had a higher concentration of soldiers. There was no moon that night, which worked to Kazama's advantage, who preferred to move in the shadows. All of these details were part of the plan which Jichirou had helped in orchestrating. Like a gust of wind, he entered the royal tent. He scanned his surroundings. The tent was filled with silk cushions and bolsters. The smell of roasted meat almost made Kazama smack his lips. He tiptoed past the naked women, lying comatose on the cushions after what must have been another night of debauchery for the Emperor's pleasure. He picked up a fruit knife from a table that was overflowing with food of all sorts, grapes, pomegranates, melons, honey, jams, skewers of unknown meats, breads and…Kazama looked away. His hand had already plucked a grape and transported it to his mouth, much to his dismay. As he chewed on the juicy fruit which burst on his tongue, he opened the door to the inner tent where the Emperor snored soundly. The Emperor lay on the royal bed, flat on his back. Besides the emperor's table was a black crystal flask with a small lock on it. Kazama knew it was a bad idea to waste time on the flask. But the lock, it tempted him. Also, the grape had left a sour taste in his throat and some expensive wine would certainly help alleviate the discomfort.

Kazama dropped the knife and stealthily rifled through the drawers for the key but couldn't find anything of use. The Emperor was lost in blissful sleep. Now's my chance, Kazama thought, looking back at the knife. But his body had other plans. Before he knew what he was doing, his hand reached inside the sleeping Emperor's tunic and plucked a tiny key out from his necklace.

The emperor merely swatted his chest and went back to his snores.

Kazama tried the key inside the lock and he could feel its tiny bolts turning. He covered the lock in his palms to muffle the click.

The aroma that came out of the flask was intoxicating. It smelled of roses and cinnamon and…it smelled a bit like rotting corpses. Kazama wondered if it was a good idea to drink whatever was inside, but the flask was already at his lips and thick dark liquid poured into him. He felt incredibly warm at first and then incredibly cold. He shivered. And then he took another gulp. He felt as if his body was splitting into two. His vision blurred and he saw four hands where there should have been two. It was a funny sight.

Suddenly, the inner door banged open and soldiers poured in. One enthusiastic soldier smashed Kazama's wrist with the flat of his sword and the black flask along with it. Black liquid splattered everywhere. The Emperor woke up in a fit and started shouting gibberish. Before Kazama could react, a heavy blow knocked the consciousness out of him.

When he came to, it was almost sunset. He had passed out for a majority of the day thanks to the strange wine and the concussion he had received. Someone splashed water onto his head. He looked below and only saw blackness. He realized that he was kneeling by the edge of the well he had spent four years digging—"The Gateway to Hell". His hands were bound tightly behind his back and his broken wrist was swollen from the blow he had received the night before. Hundreds of soldiers were lined around the perimeter of the well. There were hundreds of crows that sat around its edges too.

He looked to his right and saw Jichirou also bound and kneeling beside him. They must've found out. He looked to his left, expecting to see Shinji. But instead, it was the soldier who had knocked the flask from his hand. Also bound and kneeling.

"Your plan has failed!" shouted the fat Emperor from behind them.

"You planned to assassinate the messenger of God himself? Do you not know that I have been tasked the sacred duty of leading man into the new age? Your cowardice and irreligion has cost humanity hundreds of years of hard work! Do you understand? You drank the sacred elixir which was to be my means of communing with the God of Death himself! You tiny insects! Do you realize what you have done? Bring the other man."

Shinji was brought to the edge of the well. He looked at Kazama, sobbing. Guilt and tears fell from his eyes into the abyss before them.

"You will tell the others of what happened here today. Your life will be spared for your act of service. Do you understand?"

"Yes, my lord. Thank you my lord", sobbed Shinji.

Kazama understood what Shinji had done. He had bartered Kazama's and Jichirou's lives for the lives of the prisoners he loved. And the prisoners loved Shinji. Kazama bore him no ill will. He was only saddened by the thought that Jichirou would have to face the same fate as himself. His arms though, writhed fiercely against the rope and his swollen wrist began to bleed. His body received a swift blow from behind to behave itself.

"Throw the first one in", the Emperor commanded.

Kazama went tumbling into the darkness.

Let go of me, his body said as he fell. But this is our fate, his soul objected.

Kazama flew a downward flight through the well and realized how deep it was. The mouth of the well went from being a moon in the sky to a tiny pin-prick of light.

He landed crashing onto the floor. Bones exploded and launched themselves out of his body. An incredible pain followed the initial shock of the fall. Kazama's body let out a blood curdling cry. All the crows lining the side of the well crowed in unison and swooped into its depths.

The sun set. It was the twilight hour.

What are you doing, Kazama's soul asked.

His body merely howled.

The crows descended on him and started tearing his flesh into pieces.

Something shifted inside him.

Kazama's body tore ravenously into the crows that were in turn feasting on him. His soul looked on in horror.

Body and soul screamed in unison. The skies erupted with blue lightning. In a flash, Kazama saw a blue being that rode atop an enormous black buffalo. The being appeared as a man who had four hands and two legs. He was adorned in a golden armour and had dazzling blue skin. In one hand he held a golden mace. In another hand he held a lasso. The third and fourth hand he used to dismount the buffalo and land next to Kazama.

The being leaned beside him and whispered something in his ear.

Kazama screamed with the joy and horror of the knowledge he received. The soul understood but the body refused. They tore themselves apart from each other. Body abandoned soul. Soul abandoned body.

The world shattered.

A beam of light erupted from the well and blinded anyone foolish enough to look inside. The well, the forest and everyone inside, disappeared off the face of the earth.

34. Reunification

The being of light and being of darkness embrace one another. The being of darkness screams in agony. The being of light screams in sorrow.

Energy flows out in all directions. Everything else begins to flow in. The walls of the Well of Memories begin to crumble. Cracks open beneath my feet. The universe of stars that was above me is being sucked into the vortex that has been created by the merging of The Master and Kazama. Body and soul reunite after several millennia. The ground beneath me tilts and I'm flung through the air. I see a tornado of dust and feathers and blood. I feel the air itself being sucked out of my lungs. The tornado gets sucked into the vortex of darkness and light. All the blue stars converge into a single point. For a moment, there is only darkness. And then everything explodes.

White hot light ejects me violently from the mouth of the well. I see myself flying over Tochuu. Every single house has been flattened by the sheer force of the eruption. I fall crashing through the trees and land violently in a thicket of dense shrubbery. Through the trees I see blue light erupting into the sky, landing in gigantic balls of blue flame that begin to engulf the forest. The blue flames spread swiftly all around me. No smoke comes from the flames but everything it touches begins to burn. I see flaming blue orbs, zigzagging their way through the forest. The Aoirei have abandoned The Village of Lost Souls. I get up on my feet and start hobbling away from the flames too.

An eldritch rumble fills the sky. I can't tell if its laughter or moaning or just thunder. I see a line of blue flames in front of me. It's the shimenawa rope my mother and I once hung shide strips on. I crawl underneath it, feeling the blue heat coming off it on my back.

Once I am outside, I start running. I sprint through the forest, trampling anything in my way. I swat aside leaves and branches and vines that try to stop me. I sprint past Ganesh who waves to me from inside a bus. I wave back but I keep running. I see Gulmohar buds falling from the trees. I trample over them and keep running. I see hundreds of tall metal gates, side by side, covered in vines. I sprint and climb on top with ease and jump over them. I see Johnny, naked and crying under a tree.

"I looked inside. I saw the darkness inside you", I say to him as I run right past him.

I see my step-father standing next to Doctor Zhao, both of them shouting for me to stop. But I keep running. I see Jin running alongside me. He hands me a rose and runs away from me. The rose disappears in my hand. I see Jojo running besides me and I start crying. He has his arms outstretched. I stretch my arms out too and pick him up. He disappears inside me. I keep on running. Up ahead I see the figure of a young woman. She's dressed in an icy blue yukata with azure maple leaf patterns on it. The maple leaves are connected to each other through intertwining blue stems, threading their way through each other, wrapping themselves around the thin frame of the girl. She's not that tall, but her posture is straight and commanding.

I stop dead in my tracks.

Megumi looks at me.

"Don't stop for anything, Kiku!" she shouts, "Don't stop for anything!"

I let out a cry. I feel the words bubbling up inside me that my soul know to be true—

"I love you!"

Then I run full sprint and pass straight through her.

I run and I run and I run.

I run until I run into a body of water and fall face first into it. I sputter and spit the cold water out. Behind me I hear the ringing of a bicycle bell.

"Are you ok?" the voice asks in Japanese.

It's a policeman.

"Where am I?" I ask him.

"You are in Abashiri Lake. Do you need help?" He asks as he's dismounting from his bicycle.

I look up at the blue-grey sky. I can see some stars through the clouds. Behind the trees I see the colour of orange emerging.

I ran all the way back to Abashiri.

35. Missing Person

Local Woman Disappears Under Mysterious Circumstances

Abashiri, October 4—Police are investigating the mysterious disappearance of Abashiri resident, Megumi Amemori, 28 years old. The prime suspect in the case, Kiku Mukherjee, 32 years old, has been detained by officials for further questioning. He is a Singaporean tourist who has been in Japan for the past six weeks and was last seen at Ms. Amemori's work place. They are believed to be in a romantic relationship.

Police have requested residents to come forward if they have any information on Ms. Amemori's whereabouts.

36. Two Tickets

I accidentally bought two tickets to Hakata. I don't know what I was thinking. I guess I'm still getting used to the ticketing machines in Japan. I suppose I could talk to a station attendant and pretend not to know Japanese to try and get a refund. But then, I have a five hour train journey ahead of me and I don't mind the extra seat.

It's a beautiful spring morning in Tokyo. I stretch myself to relax and see the bustling crowds go about their day. I haven't had a moment's rest to myself in the past few months. I quit my previous job in Singapore and joined a tech start-up in Tokyo that lets me work remotely. I shuttle back and forth between Tokyo and Abashiri. The police are happy with my level of cooperation with regards to Megumi's disappearance even though they're still suspicious of me. I try to hide my frustration from them. Often, I feel like screaming, "I would like to know too where she is! Last I saw her, we were inside a deep well that exploded like a volcano in a village that exists in a different dimension. If it still exists that is. I can't even hold a funeral for her. I have to pretend she's still alive and missing!"

I cry at night, when I think about her. I laugh at odd times during the day, remembering her quick wit, and then I cry some more. I didn't realize I had so many tears inside me. Years of numbness haven't prepared me for the range of emotions I feel every day these days.

I'm standing on the train platform, my eyes brimming with tears yet again. I remember our promise, Megumi. I am leaving for Hakata. From there, I will continue my journey to Kagoshima. I have been searching online for our sky island but I haven't found anything yet. I want to see the Milky Way with you. Sometimes I wonder if the sky island is a metaphor for our own self. Maybe we're all searching for our own sky islands.

I count two, no, four Aoirei on the platform with me. The sight of them used to fill me with anxiety and fear but now it fills me with warmth and sadness. I wonder where they're headed to. Is there a place for them to go if Tochuu is no more? I decide to ask one of them if they board the same train as me.

My train arrives on time. None of the Aoirei board with me.

I place my bag in the overhead storage compartment and take the window seat. The plastic bag that contains a katsu sando and milk coffee, I place inside the seat pocket in front of me. I don't put anything on the extra seat beside me. This is Megumi's seat, I think to myself.

The shinkansen[28] shoots across the Japanese countryside. Everywhere along the way I see the magic of spring—leaves bursting with colours—pink, green, yellow, golden and everything in between. From time to time, I peek through the window on the other side of the train. When you're in the passenger seat, you tend to see only one side of the tracks. I relish my coffee and katsu sando. Mother and I used to love sharing katsu sandwiches when we travelled. My memories of our time together are still hazy, but I remember her face now. Her beautiful blue eyes. Her soft brown hair that always smelled of mint leaves. If I close my eyes and relax, I can still smell its sweet mintiness. I know her soul lies somewhere within me, protecting me.

Trees give way to forests. Forests open to show glimpses of beautiful lakes. Lakes give way to rivers. Rivers flow next to fields. Fields merge into mountains. The mountains reach for the sky. The metal train hurtles itself through it all. I put my earphones on and play Ikue Asazaki's *Hamasaki.* My eyes close and my head rests itself on the glass window. Sleep comes swiftly. Maybe I'll dream of her.

---

[28] *Shinkansen*—Bullet train

37. The Empty Seat

Kiku falls into a deep slumber.

The door connecting two compartments slides opens. So does the door connecting two worlds. A blue orb of flame floats through it. The flame blazes and sparkles above the head of a young woman. She is not dressed in grey. Her icy blue yukata has azure maple leaf patterns on it. The maple leaves are connected to each other through intertwining blue stems, threading their way through each other, wrapping themselves around her thin frame.

She sits on the empty seat next to Kiku and smiles a deep dimpled smile, looking at him.

Epilogue

The door to the apartment opens. Nakamura-san has two new visitors—a young man and a young woman. The woman looks familiar and has a blue flame on top of her head, just like him. Unlike him though, she is not grey. She's dressed in a blue yukata. The man is dressed in a black suit, hair neatly parted to the side.

"Hello, Nakamura-san", the man in black says.

"Hello", Nakamura-san replies.

"How have you been?"

Nakamura-san starts crying. He doesn't get many visitors these days.

"I am so alone. I want to leave this place."

"Where will you go, Nakamura-san?"

"I want to see my daughter", he cries.

"What's her name?"

Nakamura-san's sobs cease for a moment as he looks at the man in black, puzzled.

"I…I…she's coming home soon. But it's snowing outside."

"Do you remember her name, Nakamura-san?"

"She has a daughter. My granddaughter. She is a cute little thing. I want to cook for them."

"Do you remember your granddaughter's name?"

Nakamura-san is silent.

"Nakamura-san, do you want to leave this place?"

"Yes, I do. I'm so lonely here. I want to leave this hell."

"Then you must remember."

"I don't remember", he cries.

"Try."

"I don't remember.

I don't remember.

I don't remember", Nakamura-san cries as he falls on the floor.

"You don't remember? Or you don't want to remember?"

"I don't want to remember", he cries.

"Then you'll never leave this place."

Nakamura-san clutches his head and keeps crying dry tears. The woman in blue steps forward and touches his head.

"Father?" she asks.

"Kaori-chan?" he asks back. His crying ceases as a bolt of realization runs through him. He tries to grab onto it like trying to grab a thread passing through his fingers.

"Yes father. It is me, Kaori", the woman in blue lies.

"Kaori-chan", he sobs.

"Yes father?"

"Something happened to Aoi-chan."

"What happened to her, father?"

"I can't remember", he cries.

"Would you like to remember?"

"Yes. But, I'm afraid."

"I can help you, father. But you must want to remember. It has to be your choice."

"Yes."

"Would you like to remember?"

"Yes. I want to remember."

The woman in blue steps aside and the man in black lies down next to Nakamura-san. He stretches his arms out. Nakamura-san stretches out his own, blubbering. They embrace each other and the world goes blue.

Nakamura-san is cutting carrots for the beef curry. His kitchen smells of onions and spices. He stops his cutting to inspect one of the apples he plans to use for the curry. Apples are the secret ingredient he has never told his daughter about. His daughter loves the curry he makes. It's been snowing outside all day so she must be stuck in the snow somewhere, Nakamura-san says out loud.

Young Aoi-chan is playing with one of the apples behind him. Who's stuck in the snow, she asks her grandfather.

Your mother, you stupid girl. You're very cute but not very bright sometimes, Nakamura-san laughs as he goes back to chopping the carrots.

But mother is dead, the girl says.

Nakamura-san stops chopping.

What did you say, he asks her.

Mother is dead, the girl repeats.

What the hell do you mean by that? How could you say such an awful thing about your own mother?

But mother is dead, grandfather.

Nakamura-san swings around angrily, knife in hand. He doesn't realize how close his granddaughter is standing behind me.

Blade meets flesh.

Aoi-chan's neck slices open like an apple. Blood spurts out in an arc and lands on Nakamura-san's feet. He yelps. Knife drops to the floor. Aoi-chan follows suit.

Blood fans out of her neck in warm arcs, pooling in front of her.

Nakamura-san sees his granddaughter lying on the floor. He is lying on the floor himself. She is looking straight at him, eyes wide open. Mouth wide open. Throat wide open. His own mouth is wide open.

"I killed her."

He lies still on the floor for a few hours, staring into the space where his granddaughter had fallen many years ago. He murmurs illegible apologies to the dead. He lets out muffled screams from time to time. He cries blue tears as he battles his demons.

When he's finally silent, the woman in blue sits beside him and strokes his hair. She recites—

"You are as real as the rain that does not fall.

You live, yet you are not alive.

You seek the way because you are lost.

And in the darkness I am your guide."

Nakamura-san remains motionless on the floor, letting the blue tears flow out. When he is done, he stands up and bows his head.

"I am sorry for what I did. Please forgive me, Aoi-chan. It was a mistake. I am deeply sorry."

He bows for several minutes and then goes to the window to look outside.

"It stopped snowing", he remarks, "The sky is finally clear."

The man in black and the woman in blue smile as they hold each other's hands.

Nakamura-san walks to the door of his apartment and is about to turn the door knob when he hesitates, "Where does it lead to?"

"Outside."

"And what will I find outside?"

"The sky."

"The sky", Nakamura-san repeats.

"Would you like to go together?"

"Yes, I would."

Nakamura-san turns the door knob. The door opens. The three of them step through it together.

The End

A NOTE FROM THE AUTHOR

I hope you enjoyed my debut novel. Aoirei was originally written in a whirlwind span of 4 weeks and I poured everything I had into it. If you've enjoyed the book, I would greatly appreciate a review from you on Amazon and Goodreads as it supports new authors like me and is a major factor in generating sales.

For a "behind the scenes" on some fun facts about the book and bonus content (like the song Kiku was listening to as he fell asleep in the train), visit my blog- ranajayontheroad.com

Once again, thank you for reading. Take care and wish you an amazing journey!

www.ingramcontent.com/pod-product-compliance
Lightning Source LLC
LaVergne TN
LVHW041217150826
845673LV00001B/434

* 9 7 8 9 8 1 1 1 7 9 2 1 1 *